Budapest Artists' Club

CLAIRE DOYLE

Copyright © 2019 Claire Doyle

All rights reserved.

ISBN: 9781703378382

Note: This is a work of fiction. Names, characters, places, and incidents are a product of the author's imagination. Locales and public names are sometimes used for atmospheric purposes. Any resemblance to actual people, living or dead, or to businesses, companies, events, institutions, or locales is completely coincidental.

ALSO BY CLAIRE DOYLE

The Naked Sommelier
Hollywood Balaton

Short Stories:
Hungarian Folk Dancing For Beginners
Diving Under District VII

For the real Zoltán
You have the magic!

♥

1

There is no such thing as darkness, merely the absence of light.

I was sitting in my room in London remembering a moment from the previous week–a dance with a man, an old-fashioned dance. Zoltán and I had met before. It had been nearly twenty years and the reason I remembered was *1)* I had danced with him back then, and *2)* he was wearing Hungarian national costume. This is what had struck me. That–and the chemistry. Over all the years and all the forgetting and then I go and meet him and he has run out of money, he says. Remembering him from all those years before, I buy him a ticket. I was in Budapest and I was at the Artists' Club.

We made our way through the club to the courtyard where the band was playing. There they were–violins, violas, double bass–the troika of music. A small crowd was starting to dance *csárdás*. "Let me give you a dance lesson," said Zoltán. "I'm a dance teacher. Let me repay you," he said and he held out his hand and took mine and I felt the chemistry once more, as if from nowhere. I was unsteady on my feet, feeling dizzy sometimes. "We're all human," he said, slowing us down. "Listen to the double bass, it will help you keep time."

I trusted Zoltán. He was a careful teacher and as he took care and we spun in a circle around each other, I could hear the musicians play over his shoulder, then over mine. "I love this melody," I said.

"Me too," he replied. It was then a light came on, a curtain lifted. That bass was my clock on the wall.

The Universe was delivering me a sign. Life was not turning out as planned and those doors of fate swung open for a reason. I had to find out. I had to re-settle the past. My heart had crystallised but still, there was hope, but for what? Lot's wife turned to stone when she turned and looked back but I was no-one's wife and no-one could tell me what to do. I was Laura McLove, lover of music and dance alike. I was free to rework the past if I was ever to overcome it. A drought of musical sensation propelled me out of middle age and out of my room in London. I slipped out the door alone this time–this one last time–dance shoes in hand and headed east.

2

I never knew Budapest before 1989. I got to know it after that great year zero in time to catch a glimpse of the old days. Two towns united–Buda to the west and Pest to the east with the River Danube flowing through the centre. I lived right here on Franz Liszt Square one winter, the winter I met Sonia, Valentin, Ana, Vladimir, Lajos and–I shivered–Kati. Ibolya had funding for research and lectures at the Liszt Academy and me and Dany came too but it was Sonia we were following. We were quite a gang.

The centre of the city had a small international crowd–it still does–and I became a part of it. Elizabeth Town, or district VII as it is also known, had become a desert then, its Jewish population long disappeared or fled, its buildings abandoned, except for a few people here and there, like Lajos and his violin workshop, The Little Pipe bistro where Vladimir played piano, and the *Kádár*, the old Jewish restaurant where you can hear violin playing as you walk past but the Artists' Club here on Franz Liszt Square was my favourite. When we visited the first time, we were the only diners. I remembered the song they played there that winter. I was familiar with the tune, very familiar, but it was sung in Hungarian, *Those Were The Days*. I started humming the melody to myself as I sipped my coffee and looked across the rooftops of downtown. The sun was out and I could see the Danube glisten in the distance, the Buda hills beyond.

Budapest was a diamond in the rough. It took effort, or an accident, to find her and when you found her, she was yours and you were hers forever. She was the heart of Europe but the thing about a heart is a heart can be broken. And the thing about diamonds? I drifted back to the events nearly twenty years ago. I could never have predicted any of it.

♫ ♫ ♫ ♫ ♫ ♫

London–and Dany and I had had 'the talk'. We had decided to split or, rather, he had decided for both of us when the telephone rang. I picked up the receiver. I could hear the call to prayer from the Whitechapel mosque and Cosmic the donkey braying down in the yard. It was raining. It didn't look like the weather would lift all day. Spitalfields in all its glory. "Hello?"

"Laura, what are you doing this evening? You must come out with me tonight." It was Ibolya.

"Nothing. The weather's terrible. I'm not in the mood. Even the cat seems depressed …" I said. I could hear her draw on a cigarette.

"Never mind your mood. Listen, I have free tickets for a show tonight at the Ukrainian Club. You have to come."

"What's the show?" I asked. I mouthed Ibolya's name in silence to Dany as he came into the room. He loved Ibolya and grabbed the phone from me. "Ibolya! How are you?" He clutched the telephone with both hands.

"There are some Gypsies over from Hungary–come and see them with me tonight. I've got free tickets!" she said loud enough that I could hear the conversation at the other end of the room now. "I'm coming! Laura too! I'll talk her round," said Dany. I sighed and crossed my arms and stared out at the rain holding the cat, tuning into the pit-a-pat sound on the window pane. "You know, Sam is very keen on you," said Dany, putting down the receiver.

"I know–we have a private view at The Void tonight. He's reading poems at six."

"We can do both," said Dany.

"Sam is useless. He's a drunk and he's a poet. Hopeless."

"He's the best poet I ever heard. You should think about it."

Sam was forever making up poems about me. Tonight was one of them. *Laura The Tap Breaker*, he called it. I could never be with a man like that.

That night, we met Ibolya at Holland Park tube. The Ukrainian Club was a terraced house with pillars at the front door, like many others in west London but like The Beatles house in *Help!*–appearance was deceptive. The door opened leading to a hallway, the hallway led to a concert hall with a stage. It was noisy. People were seated in rows or at a bar buying drinks. On the stage was a double bass on its side, violins and other instruments propped on chairs or on the floor. Dany was transfixed. "Have you seen that double bass bow?" he said, pointing at the bow lying on top of the bass. "It's made from a scrap of wood and tied with a knot. It's completely rustic," he said. "And look at those bass strings, they're made of gut. It's so rough!" His French accent became more pronounced the more excited he became. We took our seats shortly before the lights dimmed and the audience became quiet. The band was tuning up. It sounded like traffic. I noticed a couple to the left of the stage on the dance floor, dressed in folk costume.

Sonia's on-stage presence was staggering. He was tall with black hair, dark eyes, strong features. He was wearing a white suit with a red shirt and a white tie, a red hanky at the breast pocket and black patent loafers with gold buckles. I had never seen anything like him. I noticed a gold ring on his finger as he began to play violin unaccompanied, very slow. The violas joined in with the violin and then the double bass began last. Everything sounded out of tune like an old long-playing record played backward. "This is Transylvanian music," whispered Ibolya in my ear. "It's the real thing, you'll never hear anything better," she said as I stared at the dancers spinning on the floor. I was mesmerised by that sludge of the double bass. I wanted more as the music speeded up, then slowed down and changed. The male dancer was directing the musicians at times and, I noticed, he also controlled his partner in that spiral dance. "It's a *csárdás*," whispered Ibolya.

Afterwards the lights went on and the chairs were cleared. People hung to the corners of the room. Ibolya and I followed Dany towards the stage. He always wanted to talk to the musicians.

"I love your bass playing. Can I look at it? I'm an instrument maker," said Dany to the bass player with Ibolya translating into Hungarian. The bass player was swigging from a bottle that was wrapped in a brown paper bag and he held it out to me. "It's *pálinka*," said Ibolya. "Brandy. Have some."

"Is it safe?" I looked up and into Sonia's eyes for the first time. He had eyes dark enough to lose myself.

"It's medicine–go on, have some," he said.

"I love your music," I said as I took the small plastic water bottle to my lips and swallowed. I felt an intense burn on the back of my tongue, down my throat and the warmth spread through my chest. "I loved it. I love the bass and I love that viola. It's got three strings! I've never seen such a thing," I said. Sonia picked the instrument up from the stage.

"Here, have a look." He held the viola out to me. It was golden brown, white rosin dust lying all over the belly and the back was made of a single piece of flaming walnut. It wasn't a regular instrument, someone special had made this. "Who made it? It's beautiful," I said. I held the viola out to Dany who was by now swigging *pálinka* even though he was teetotal. "Dany makes musical instruments. Lutes and things."

"Really?" Sonia looked to Dany. "I have a friend in Budapest, he made it especially for me and especially to play the three strings only. It's his own design."

"Is that where you live? Budapest?" I asked.

"I'm from Transylvania but I stay in Budapest for work."

"We've never been to Budapest," said Dany. "Ibolya is from Budapest."

"Hello Ibolya," said Sonia.

"Good to see you Sonia. The music was fantastic as usual." She was lighting a cigarette.

"You know each other?" I said.

"We're neighbours," said Sonia. "We both have a place on Franz Liszt Square. You should come to Budapest, it's a great town."

"Why can't you play with us?" said Dany. "We have a gig early next year but we don't have a bass player. Can you play bass too? We can split the money four ways." Dany was looking at Ibolya.

"I never thought about it," said Ibolya blowing out some smoke. "Why didn't I think of it before? Sonia plays everything."

"We had a Swiss bass player for a while but his heart wasn't in it," I said. "We were hoping for a Swiss tour, in truth."

"Bloody Swiss. Five hundred years of peace and all they gave us is the Eurovision Song Contest," said Ibolya. "As if we didn't have other things to contend with in 1956."

"I could play with you but I have a condition," said Sonia. "Perhaps you can help me with something?"

"What's that?" I asked.

"I want my grandfather's viola back."

"Why? Where is it?" asked Dany. "Romania. The communists took it. I've tried the official channels but they don't recognise my claim. They hate the Gypsies. They say I have no proof that it belongs to my family. So it hangs in a case in the Romanian National Museum of Agricultural History."

"Why is it in an agricultural museum?" said Dany looking perplexed.

"It's a Gypsy instrument ..." he began.

"They haven't a clue about music," Ibolya interrupted.

"They confiscated it in 1960 from my grandfather and since the changes in 1989, I've been trying to get it back. They say I have no proof."

"So how do you know it's yours?" I asked.

"My mother told me before she died. She said, if there's one thing you must do it is to return that viola to our family. I asked her why it was in the agricultural museum?"

"Why is it in the agriculture museum?" said Dany again.

"I don't know–just then she died."

"But how could we help?" I asked. "What could we possibly do?"

"They might take you more seriously. You're an instrument maker right?" He looked at Dany. Dany nodded. "And Ibolya, you work at the Liszt Academy sometimes, no?"

"Soon, actually," she said, blowing smoke into the air. "I like to call it the Ministry of Music."

"You could open doors for me. It rightfully belongs to me. I've seen the viola ..."

"How do you know it *is* yours?" said Dany.

"There's a Roma wheel carved on the button on the back." He picked up his violin and demonstrated with his little finger, rotating it in a circle on the wood where the

Roma wheel would be carved. "It's very faint now but you can see it there. That's how I know." The band was tuning up again on the stage. "I have to play again. Come and join me in the wild east," he said, as he picked up his violin and bow once more. He was beautiful. Dany and I may have been falling out of love but now we were falling in love with Sonia.

The music began again slowly, the lights in the room remained lit this time and the two folk dancers approached to find partners from the audience. Horrified, I realised one was coming towards me and he held out his hand. I shook my head. No! I was not a dancer–no, not folk dancing! Not in front of all these people–no! But he took my hand and I found myself the centre of attention on the dance floor whilst he spun me around in the middle of the room as if to introduce me to the band. "Relax. Don't worry," he said. There was no way out. He held me, spun me, guided me with such confidence that I became, for those brief moments, a dancer. "Look at my shoulders. Don't take your eyes away from my shoulders and you will be fine," he said. The chemistry was immediate. What just happened? And then we stopped. "I have to teach some others," he said as he lifted my hand and kissed it, displaying the crown of his hat like a matador. "I am Zoltán."

"I'm Laura," I replied and he walked towards another woman, leaving me on the floor as it began to fill with people. I stood watching him when Ibolya and Dany approached.

"So now you are a dancer," said Ibolya laughing.

"That was amazing."

"So we go," she said.

"Where?"

"To the wild east. I'm due for six weeks of lectures. Come with me. You can stay with me and I could even pay you a little if you help with my research. My funding from the politburo came through."

"The politburo?" said Dany.

"Europe. Brussels. I got my euros. We go." She put her cigarette to her mouth and inhaled.

"It'll be my birthday then," I said. "And Christmas …"

"And New Year, new millennium," she said. She exhaled a slow cloud of smoke then started to sing deep in her throat and threw her arm in the air as the music began and then she stopped.

"What was that song you were singing?" I asked.

"I made it up." She shrugged.

"Just like that?"

"Just like that." She waved her hand again and laughed.

And it was just like that, we defected *en masse* to Budapest.

3

Alone, I could take my time to find Zoltán. It had been two weeks since I had seen him at the Artists' Club but nearly twenty years where life had lost its lustre and had settled into a stable, dull–and single–mediocrity. Ibolya's call had changed all that. Out of the blue, she had invited me over for the weekend and then this act of fate with Zoltán had turned into an act of destiny. I took a fancy Airbnb apartment on the square, on the top floor of number ten. It was an old-style flat with high ceilings, wooden floors, high double doors painted cream and a modern American style kitchen. Luxurious.

I opened the window that first May morning and looked down to the street. There were a few people scuttling back and forth and I could hear the clink of cups and glasses being set out in the cafes. That old song again–*Those Were The Days*–floated into my mind. I had friended Zoltán on Facebook. I could see his green light on the chat function but for some reason, he hadn't responded to my messages so when I heard the sixth district church clock strike nine, I decided to go downstairs. A thrill took me over as I descended the spiral staircase, past the broken fountain to the big wooden door and stepped out into the sunshine. It wasn't hot, not yet.

I walked around the square. The building at number thirteen was as black as ever and still maintained by heavy oak scaffold. I remembered asking Sonia about it once and even he didn't know the truth of the owner although he lived there. There was an outdoor stage being built here by Andrássy Avenue and as I crossed the square, I noticed a plaque on the wall of the Writers' Store next to the foreign exchange booth. I hadn't noticed it before. There was a dying rosette beneath. It depicted a dancing couple and the words–

'The First *Táncház*–6 May 1972'

I knew what that meant. I knew all about the *táncház*, the dance house.

I wandered past a few cafes to the blue building where Ibolya lived and there it was, the Artists' Club with its Greek pillars at the entrance. It was closed for now. I turned and looked up at the Liszt Academy, dazzling in the sunshine, now repaired by European money then I wandered into the trees and sat by the Franz Liszt statue for a time, my mind vacant. I was home. I took a seat at the Lisztró Cafe and ordered breakfast, my mind light and unburdened and stared happily into the middle distance. Now, where would I find Zoltán?

4

"I hate these modern composers," said Dany. "The invention of the piano ruined everything."

Nearly twenty years earlier, Dany and I had arrived on the square on a frozen Sunday in mid-November. Ibolya was showing us around her apartment which faced onto the music academy at the other side of the square. The living room windows on the fourth floor were level with the Liszt sculpture on the front of the building, irritating Dany, the early music freak, every time he saw it. "Stupid modern people," he would say.

"I don't know much Liszt, Ibolya," I said.

"He lived around the corner, you know." She switched on the stereo. "Here we are–Liszt lesson for you. Hungarian Rhapsody Number One. C Minor." Dany groaned.

"I recognise the music," I said. "I like it. It's–gothic?"

"It's romantic my dear."

"Is there a cross over?"

"There is no gothic–not in music."

The apartment was filled from floor to ceiling with books and there was an upright piano in the corner of the living room. The central heating was fierce and it needed to be for a Hungarian winter. "I can play on the grand piano across the road anytime," said Ibolya as we stood at the window. "Sometimes I play on Liszt's own piano over there," she said, with a nod in the direction outside. "It's easy for work to live here and I don't like to commute. It's so bourgeois." Hers was a pale blue 1960s block, socialist housing if you will, although Ibolya was anything but socialist. She had a mind of her own.

She showed Dany and I to a double bedroom at the back of the apartment. We hadn't told anyone of our discussion to split, except for poet Sam who I'd left in charge of the flat back in London. We had put everything on hold for our European adventure. In a 'post-relationship friendship' mode and with no-one around to change that, I was hoping for reconciliation. The room overlooked an inner garden with a balcony. The bed was made of dark oak and covered with a heavy patchwork quilt with big, old-fashioned white pillows. "I'm going to make us something to eat," said Ibolya, leaving us to settle in the room.

Later we sat at the living room window drinking tea and eating little pastries. "So," said Ibolya, "Sonia is living in the black building. Number thirteen. It's at the other end of the square. It's a mystery to me that place. I don't know why it remains so derelict. Andrássy Avenue is a world heritage site after all."

"Who owns it?" I said.

"Who indeed? Now, where shall we go to eat tonight?"

"Let's try the number that we have for Sonia and maybe we can meet up," said Dany, his mouth full of crumbs. "But first we better turn down the music." Ibolya had an old-style green plastic telephone with a circular dial. "It's so retro!" I said as Dany dialled the number whilst Ibolya held the receiver. I listened from across the room.

"Sonia, so you're home," said Ibolya. "We're here us three and we want to eat out tonight–where shall we go?"

"I'll be at the Artists' Club at eight," said Sonia. "I've got someone for you to meet so we can talk business. You know, the viola case."

5

The Artists' Club was on the corner of the square, bordering King Street. We walked through its pillared entrance to a 19th-century dining room with a long oak bar, oak-panelled walls, marble columns and statuettes, sparkling chandeliers. I felt like I was stepping back in time. There was piano music playing. I had heard that melody before. It stopped me in my tracks. I knew that song, it sounded Russian. Sonia got up from his chair when he saw us and walked towards us. "Sonia!"

"Laura! So good to see you!" He took my right hand, "*Csókolom*," he said and kissed it. Ibolya held out her hand. "*Csókolom*," he said again and kissed her hand too.

"It means 'I kiss your hand,' said Ibolya to me. "It's the old way."

"I could get used to this," I said as Sonia helped me take off my coat and hat and hung them on the coat stand. "What's that music? It sounds Russian," I said.

"That's Vladimir. He usually plays at The Little Pipe but sometimes here too," said Sonia. "It's an old Russian folk song."

"Actually, it's an adaption of an old Russian folk song," said Ibolya. She started to sing. "*Those were the days ...*"

"Ohmigod! It's Mary Hopkins! No wonder it's so familiar! It's fabulous!" Dany frowned at me and gestured for me to be quiet. "Oh, don't worry," said Ibolya, stopping her singing now. "It's not a performance."

We took a table beneath a naked cherub statue. Around the panelled walls were portraits of the great and the good, all men, all with flamboyant neckties, all artists I supposed. All great thinkers. All serious men with serious thoughts and serious work. "What happened to the women in those days? It's like we've been wiped from the slate," I said, picking up a menu.

"Not anymore," said Ibolya.

"History is full of people trying to wipe each other from the slate," said Sonia. "Or from the state."

"We have a new friend," said Ibolya. "Good evening to you." I looked up from the menu and standing before us at the top of the table was a short man in a dark overcoat and hat with a bright red scarf around his neck. His eyes were the colour of walnuts.

"Lajos! Everyone, Lajos Schunde, an old family friend. He is going to help us with our venture. He is the best violin maker I know," said Sonia getting up to give his friend a hug.

"Good evening," said Lajos to us all, untying his scarf to reveal a red bow at his neck.

"I make instruments too," said Dany, holding out his hand with excitement. "Lutes and baroque guitars. I finished my studies six months ago. I'm so pleased to meet you. Can I visit your workshop? I still make my instruments at home. I've made some violins too for practice …"

"We have all evening to talk about music and instruments but I'm hungry. And I'm thirsty," said Lajos as he took off his coat, hat, gloves and scarf.

"Let's order some wine. Let's have some *pezsgő*!" said Ibolya. "Champagne all round!"

"Excellent idea," said Lajos. "We all need a little sparkle in mid-winter."

Three hours, three bottles of *pezsgő* and five servings of *gulyás* later we had a plan for the viola. Sonia had passed around a photograph he had taken of the instrument in its museum case.

"I need three weeks to construct the instrument, Lajos. I just need some wood, some bench space but the thing I'll need most help with is the varnish," said Dany.

"I am at your service," said Lajos. "We can start experimenting on that when we get a better photograph. Then, when the instrument is complete, we can varnish it straight away."

"Is this legal?" I said. "To swap one instrument for another like this?"

"Who even cares?" said Ibolya. "We've all seen the picture. It's not as if anyone cares about the thing. It's not worth money and there are a ton of these folk instruments around Romania. Who knows why it's been stuck in that institute for so long? I suspect it's sheer Romanian bloody-mindedness and–she took a sip of champagne –they don't care about the Gypsies so they won't help you, Sonia. But I care and I shall help. Besides, I love a little intrigue." She took a long inhale of her cigarette then blew her smoke in the air. "Tomorrow, first thing, in the office, I will telephone Romania. Of course, things can be closed on a Monday in Romania …"

"*Luni inchis*," said Sonia.

"Exactly."

"Monday closed."

"I will make the contact and then I will draft a letter to visit and view and measure the instrument with Dany. I see no reason why we cannot go by the end, maybe even the middle of this week. It will require just an overnight stay for myself and Dany. We will be back in time for your birthday, Laura."

"You won't need me?" I said. "What will I do?"

"Why don't you learn to play the viola?" said Sonia. I have a spare that I'm not using right now. If you work at it every day, you'll pick up some basics pretty quick. Come to me in the morning and we'll get started."

"And you can tell me what you learn," said Ibolya. "I'll feed it into my talk on New Year's Eve. I'll sort out some euros for you and Dany tomorrow from my funding."

It was close to midnight when we walked to Lajos' workshop on Klauzal Square. "I forgot to feed the cat," he said. Frost sparkled on the violin sign above our heads as Lajos unlocked the heavy door that opened onto an inner courtyard although his workshop faced the street. "Good for business," he said. "People can pop in anytime. Some of my customers are good friends." He turned on the lights. There were violins and pieces of violins everywhere, on the worktops, hanging from the ceiling. One wall was lined with tools and there were three wooden benches. "And here is Bartók who looks after the workshop every night," said Lajos picking up a large black purring cat from the floor wearing a diamanté collar. "Isn't she beautiful? I love Bartók. When I run into difficulty with an instrument or a customer, I pick her up and she makes things alright again."

"Can I?" I said, holding out my hands for Bartók. The cat was heavy, purring and sleek as a panther.

"I'm here from eight-thirty until six every day except between one and two when I have lunch at the *Kádár*, if you want to see me. If I'm not here, I'm there. It's here on Klauzal Square," he said as he filled Bartók's bowl with food. I placed Bartók back on the floor to purr around Lajos' ankles.

6

Next morning, I headed across the square to number thirteen. Homeless men were sheltering beneath the scaffold as I entered the large black door through to an inner courtyard with a fountain and a violinist sculpture at the centre. I decided to climb the stairs to Sonia's apartment in case the lift didn't work.

At the top floor, I walked along the corridor and found Sonia unlocking a gate. He was wearing a shiny emerald shirt with black trousers, his hair was slicked back as usual and on his feet were black slip-on slippers. "My God but you are stylish," I said. "You're in a league of your own." He grinned.

"Welcome," he said. "This is home." I walked through the little gates at his open doorway and stepped inside. "It's beautiful," I said. "Who would think it from the way the building is on the outside?" I stepped into a high ceilinged corridor with wooden flooring. There were floor to ceiling double doors to every room. The place was spacious beyond belief. The living room had a modern kitchen in the corner and two black leather sofas. "Black leather! I would never have guessed it!" I said. The windows overlooked the square and a curtain made of deep blue threads hung against them allowing you to see across the rooftops to the

Buda Hills. A crystal chandelier hung from the centre of the ceiling. "It's gorgeous!"

"I'm a lucky man," said Sonia. "Now I have a gift for you to practise with," he said taking a viola out of a black case. "This is yours for as long as you are here in Budapest. It will get you started. Here," he said. I took the viola.

"It's beautiful. It's yours?"

"Sure but I have a lot of instruments. Sometimes I buy and sell them with Lajos. I always have something around. This one isn't valuable but it has a good sound. It's one of the better ones from the factory in Romania. I tuned it already so we are ready to go and here is a bow.

"But it's a cello bow."

"How else can you play three strings at once? I rosined it for you and the first lesson is, can you hold it without dropping it?" I took the viola from his hand and held it sideways, supporting it with my wrist and my chin, the way I had seen others do. I picked up the bow with my right hand and made a dreadful noise as I played the bow over the open strings. The viola didn't wobble but then I wasn't holding a chord so I could grip it tightly. Sonia watched with amusement. "If there was a cat in here, she would have fled," he said.

"If it's not written down, then how do you learn this music?" I asked.

"By copying."

"It's that easy?"

"Sure, it's the best thing to do at first, after that you learn the rules."

"And what are the rules?"

"It depends on what you want to learn. Just because something isn't written down doesn't mean it doesn't have rules. Once you learn the rules, you internalise it and on stage you go," he said. "One other thing–you have to learn the style. That's the difficult bit, but even that has rules–after that, it's up to you."

He showed me three basic chords–G, D, and A and on a piece of paper he drew three lines for the three viola strings and a dot where my fingers should be placed for each chord. It was tough work. Holding the viola alone would take time. This was a whole new way of looking at the world.

It was fun to spend alone time with Sonia but he was a master musician and I asked him why he bothered with me. "We made a deal, no? I like you. Why not?" I agreed to return the following morning and practised all afternoon in Ibolya's flat until my fingers hurt. It was getting dark at four o'clock when Ibolya and Dany came home.

"We're leaving on Wednesday! Florin Ionesco is meeting us at the train station in Cluj-Napoca!" said Dany, his French accent stronger in his excitement.

"Who is Florin Ionesco? He sounds like a surrealist," I said.

"I think you mean absurdist," said Ibolya. "He works at the Romanian National Museum of Agricultural History in *Kolozsvár*, or Cluj as they say in Romania. He was surprised to get a call from Hungary to view and measure that viola. He said that there had been one or two people interested in the last year–which must have been Sonia–and he was happy to help. Kati did most of the talking."

"Kati?"

"My assistant. She speaks Romanian. She's Hungarian but was born there in Transylvania like lots of Hungarians. And one more thing ..." Ibolya reached into her handbag and pulled out an envelope. "I have a present from Brussels. They're euros so you'll have to get them changed to Hungarian forint. Write down every day what you learn from Sonia and I can include it in my research."

7

Tuesday morning and I was back at number thirteen. Sonia was wearing a cream shirt with brown horse motifs all over. He pulled a red ribbon from out of his pocket. "This is for you," he said. He took the viola from my hands and tied the ribbon in a bow around the neck. "Now you can hang it on the wall. And when you see the viola on your wall every day, you will pick it up more and begin to fall in love with your instrument. This is very important." He showed me three more chords–E, C and F–and wrote them again on paper. Over coffee later I asked him, "How long have you been playing Sonia?"

"All my life. I cannot remember a time when I didn't play music. I started pretending with wooden sticks instead of a violin and bow when I was very young and by the time I was six, I had a small violin and went to work with my father and his band. It has never been any other way."

"Are you married?"

"No. but I was engaged to a girl once …" His voice trailed off.

"What happened?"

"She was Romanian, not Roma so it would never have worked," he said. "I left Romania after that."

By Wednesday, I was making progress with the chords. "It's true what you said about the viola, about hanging it on the wall. It was the first thing I saw this morning when I woke up. I love it though I think it was a little early for Ibolya when I started playing in the apartment." Ibolya, Dany and Kati had taken the train to Transylvania early morning. I would be alone that night.

Sonia played a simple melody on the violin whilst I tried to keep up and accompany him. "You need to learn to dance," said Sonia. "It will help with the music and give you something to think about whilst everyone is away. I suggest we go to the *Fonó* tonight."

That evening, with Sonia dressed in a grey pinstripe suit, coat and fedora, violin case in hand, we took a yellow Tram 47 from Deák Square and trundled across the Danube on the Freedom Bridge to Buda. We clattered around the Gellért Hotel, chugged along Béla Bartók Street and down a long straight road. The *Fonó* was a modern build with a large dance hall and stage. I joined a dance class. I watched and I copied the teacher, as we all did in a big circle in the room. Finally, I gave up when we had to dance with partners. It got too difficult. A free dance took off later by the bar with live music. I ordered a beer in English when a man approached. "I am Valentin and I am from Romania. You are British aren't you?"

"Scotland. My name is Laura." I held out my hand and we shook. But you have an American accent."

"I lived in New York but now I live here. And you?"

"I'm visiting. I met Sonia in London–do you know him?" I pointed to Sonia as he talked with a man at the other end of the bar. "He invited us over and … it's a little complicated. I'm staying down at Franz Liszt Square," I said. "It's lovely there."

"You live by the Artists' Club!" Another woman was at our side now, younger with long dark hair and brown eyes. "And you are?" I said.

"I'm Ana. This is my dad. I know Sonia, I've danced with him before. Do you dance?"

"No, I tried for the first time tonight. It's hard, never mind that I'm trying to learn that viola with three strings as well. Sonia is giving me lessons."

"I've been dancing since I got here a year ago," she said. "Sometimes I think I'll take up the violin too."

"Do you want to dance Laura?" asked Valentin, holding out his hand as the band had begun to tune up again. "This is an easy one to start with. I can show you." I looked at Ana.

"Go on Laura, he's not a bad dancer my father," she said.

On the dance floor, I placed my hands on Valentin's shoulders and he placed his hands on my hips. Other couples were around us. "Start with your left leg and go backward," said Valentin. I watched another couple close by for a few bars of music. "Ready?" he said.

"OK" I replied.

"One, two, one-two-three. One, two, one-two-three," said Valentin and on the third one, two, one-two-three, I stepped backward in time to the music and then forwards again with another one, two, one-two-three and on we went. Time and timing. Was my timing wrong in the past? Clock time didn't exist in this music, you could put away that metronome, the double bass is what I had to listen to with its easy swing. This was my body clock on the dance floor.

Next steps followed the same rhythm but Valentin swung me round to the right on a one, two, one-two-three and then back to my starting place. Around to the left and back to the starting place. "OK Laura, next we are dancing a simple *csárdás*. "Stay hold of my shoulders." We were standing side by side to each other now–I faced one direction and he faced another. I was so busy listening to instructions that I could barely hear any music. My hands remained on his shoulders, his hands on my hips.

"Start with your right foot. One, two, one-two-three," and at that we began to circle around each other in a *csárdás*. "One, two, one-two-three. One, two, one-two-three," chanted Valentin. He drew me into his orbit, an orbit unfamiliar, unpleasant at first until I got the hang of it. And then I got the hang of it. And then I got the pleasure of it. And I could still hear the music, and I danced. It was a trickier step than the previous one but even so, I got the hang of it and I was starting to understand why Valentin had that name. He was masterful on the dance floor and our movements and changes of direction were seamless. I saw Sonia in the distance, dancing with Ana. They made a great pair.

Sonia and I got back to Franz Liszt Square at 2 am. We took the late-night tram that crossed back over Freedom Bridge and walked from Oktogon. "Did you know this was once called Mussolini Square?" said Sonia. "And then they called it November 7 Square for fifty years. Now it's back to the original name."

"Oktogon–it's not very poetic is it?" I said, as we walked past Liszt's statue, lit up in the night. The square was empty as we stopped at my door. "I'll see you tomorrow for a viola lesson. How about 12?"

"OK."

"Sleep tight Laura. You want to watch out for that Valentin," he said as he kissed me goodbye on either cheek. "He's quite a charmer."

8

Project Zoltán and I decided to make a plan for the week.

He would be at the music pubs, of that I was sure but only on the nights where there was a live band and a dance. I got online and discovered two bars with live music, the *Szimpla* Garden and the Grid Garden. There was the *Fonó* as usual, and, of course, the Artists' Club. I determined to go to all of them. Something would have to give.

I had a look at the news online. A referendum on Europe was coming up. I didn't believe in referenda, they were a fools' game. The real deals were done behind closed doors. In or out? I had voted with my feet. There were pressing questions to answer, like, could I make Zoltán fall for me? Had twenty years of my own personal dark ages been in vain? A referendum could never fix my life, only I could and if I couldn't, at least I could come here and enjoy the music. With my EU passport, I had ninety days to get the hell into Schengen. And then I could leave. Or remain.

I was single in a single market–an older woman, still feeling young. Where would I find Zoltán? It was noon now. I took the lift down to the square and walked across to the Artists' Club. "Valentin! It's Laura! Look at you! You've got gray hair!"

"Scottish Laura! You still look so beautiful!"

"You haven't changed then …" I said, as we hugged each other. "I heard you worked here?"

"I manage the bar. The place went private a few years go, everything has changed. It's better but in some ways … I liked the old days. And you, are you on holiday?"

"In a way," I said. "I met this dancer called Zoltán …"

"There's quite a few Zoltáns in Budapest."

"He's very tall and he always wears a hat," I said.

"I know that Zoltán," he said.

"I'd like to see him again."

"Then we shall find him. Together. I will help."

"And Ana? How is Ana?"

"She is back in New York. She returned to study music in the end and to see her mother."

"I can't believe it's you!"

"Listen, I have to work now …" Valentin was looking around the dining room. It was a Cuban bar now and it was filling up. It was still magnificent.

"I made a plan for the week. The *Fonó* …"

"Of course …"

"And the ruin pubs with the dance nights. I want to hang out in the bars, I want to find Zoltán there."

"Good thinking. Now we are in business. We have a plan and we will execute the plan. Take a seat outside. You never were here in the good weather and I will bring you some lunch–on the house."

We walked through the bar to the courtyard garden and I took a seat in the shade. "Oh, it's so lovely!"

"House special is chicken *paprikás* today and I will bring you salad and a little champagne. I remember you liked *Törley*."

"My first *Törley* in twenty years!"

I sipped on the cold champagne as Valentin brought me lunch and as I kicked off my sandals, Valentin said, "I have something else special for you today." I heard a Hungarian woman's voice sing over the sound system, '*Aki A Szép Napok*'–*Those Were The Days*.

These were the days, I thought as I ate lunch, said a goodbye to Valentin for now and returned to the apartment where I fell into a deep *siesta*.

9

Thursday at noon and back to Sonia's. He greeted me in high waisted black trousers and a shiny shirt with a wild black and brown zig-zag pattern. Today was for bowing techniques. How to bow the length of the bow on all three viola strings at the same time. Sometimes I stopped the bowing mid bow-stroke for an off-beat but I still had trouble holding the viola and co-ordinating the movements.

Afterwards, I walked through the square and sat on the bench in front of the Franz Liszt statue with his giant hands held to the sky. I was in no mood to spend the afternoon practising indoors. The days were getting shorter and I needed some light. I returned the viola to the flat and took a walk up Andrássy Avenue into town. Christmas lights were going up. God, how I hated Christmas! I thought of Dany and his age. I couldn't blame him for wanting to separate, he was too young. Had he been out to use me all along? I walked all the way into town until I found myself on Oktober VI Street. I had a browse in Bestsellers, the English bookshop then headed for the Danube. The rush hour was beginning when I finally turned away from the river, a sprinkle of snow fell on my face and I looked up beneath an orange streetlight and there were heavenly flakes everywhere. I felt redeemed and, unusual for me in those days, I jumped on a tram to take me back to the square.

10

Friday–my birthday–and Sonia came to the blue building for a change. He arrived in a herringbone overcoat and a trilby hat carrying his violin. There was a light dusting of snow on his coat and fedora. "You look great," I said. Today's shirt was black with little black cats on. He tuned my instrument to his, as usual, plucking at each viola string and twiddling with the pegs. Then he held it sideways and played chords C and G, then E and A. "I haven't learned any minor chords yet," I said.

"We can play all day on major. Some of this music only has major accompaniment–but the tunes can be minor."

"So that's why it sounds so strange," I said.

Our routine was the same. Over and over with those chords to a simple melody he played, over and over with the bowing, stopping and starting, playing faster. A strange wall of sound began to emanate from my instrument, not dissimilar to a church organ. Sonia stopped his violin. "I'm beginning to sound like a sparrow in a rush," he said.

He started again slowly this time. It was sad. He called out some chords for me to follow and after five minutes we stopped again because the telephone rang. "You'll be on stage in no time," he said as I picked up the green plastic receiver.

"Hello?" It was Dany in Romania.

"Laura! We've done it! I've got lots of photos of the viola! And I measured it! How are you? Happy birthday!"

"Sonia is here–we're both great! So when are you back?"

"I'm coming back tomorrow," he said.

"But it's my birthday ..."

"There's a music event here tonight and we don't want to miss it. Ibolya and Kati are staying ..."

"Oh." I looked at Sonia. "But it's my birthday! We were going to The Little Pipe! I booked it!"

"I know, I know, I'm sorry! But we can go out on Saturday night instead! We all want to stay!"

"They're staying another night," I said to Sonia as I shrugged my shoulders. "There's a music night tonight, apparently."

"So how is everything with the instrument?" said Sonia.

"Tell Sonia everything is going to plan. I can't wait to see you both and tell you all about it but I have to go now. I will bring you a present from Romania," said Dany. I put down the phone.

"They must like Romania," said Sonia. "It *is* an interesting place."

"Perhaps I should have gone with them," I said. "It's my birthday." I plucked each of the viola strings one after the other. G, D and A.

"Well, as you're now alone this evening, let's go to the Artists' Club. I'm playing in the band tonight."

"Oooo!" I strummed those three strings together now.

"And bring your instrument. If you want to be a real musician, you've got to get with the band."

"That's scary," I said.

"I'll help you, don't worry. It'll be great. the Artists' Club is called that for a reason. It's a great place and we can stay up late–I know how much you like that."

"I'd better cancel the Little Pipe. I really wanted to go there, it's so famous."

"My grandfather knew that guy, Rezső Seress, the one who wrote the song," said Sonia.

"Really?" I replied.

"Sure, he never left the seventh district for ten years. And he refused to go to America to collect his royalties. My grandfather often went to see him when he was in town. He said it made a change for him–listening to popular piano music and a little bit of Rachmaninoff and Chopin, Brahms and Liszt. He liked it. And he liked him."

We started again on those damn chords. Sonia listened to what I had learned so far then wrote out more chords for me and a pattern to learn them. He showed me a new bowing technique–a long bow stroke as an off-beat–and how to change chord shapes with the left hand at the same time. It was a slow process, this three-stringed viola, but a hypnotic one. I was glad for Sonia in the absence of Dany. He treated me as a fellow musician and I would always be grateful to him for that. And what is a musician if they never play in public? "I'll bring the viola tonight," I said.

That night I walked down the four flights of stairs from Ibolya's, viola in hand. I heard the front gate open and close. The lift passed me as I descended from the first floor to the ground. I hesitated for a moment. Should I be afraid at ten o'clock at night? I went out to the square and found a crowd outside the music academy. A concert had recently finished. I saw a woman pull her coat around her, her diamanté necklace sparkling in the lights. I entered the Artists' Club feeling like a real musician. The first people I saw were Valentin and Ana. "Hey, you two!" I joined them at a table. "It's my birthday!"

"Have some wine?" said Valentin. "This is a Bull's Blood from Eger. It's table wine really," he said as he turned over a small tumbler that was on the table. The tables were set for food.

"Sonia's playing tonight. I've been getting lessons," I said.

"Is that why you've brought your viola?" asked Ana.

"I'm not sure I'll use it. Dany has abandoned me in favour of Romania for another night so now you are my guests for dinner." I picked up a menu and gave them one to read between them. "Go on, have what you want. I'm paying. We're on a euro junket."

"We're going to dance so we could eat later," said Ana, not wanting to upset me.

"Then it's time for *pezsgő*," I said. I ordered a bottle of *Törley* and three retro champagne glasses. I also ordered cabbage salad and *pogácsak*, little scones, to keep my hunger at bay. The waiter arrived with the wine, opened it and poured for us, leaving the bottle in an ice bucket by the side of the table.

"Gosh, I feel like a queen here," I said.

"And I'm a princess," said Ana.

"Then I am king for the night," said Valentin and we clinked glasses together us three.

"I'm pissed off Dany isn't here. I wanted to go to The Little Pipe."

"Everything happens for a reason, Laura. Besides it's his first time in Romania–he wants to make the most of it. Especially if he meets some of the Gypsy musicians there," said Valentin.

"I should have gone too," I said looking around the room. The club was getting busy now, a convivial air prevailed. An old peasant woman was setting out textiles on a corner table as the band began to tune up, or tune out, as Ibolya called it. The music was still peculiar to my western ear. No matter, I was adjusting. Valentin stood up. "Laura, it's your birthday and we are going to dance. You will be in safe hands."

"Go on, Laura," said Ana. "It'll be fun."

"OK, but first I'm going to buy myself a birthday present," I said, nodding at the peasant woman. "I like the look of those black waistcoats." I chose a little sequinned waistcoat the woman had sewn herself. It had no lining but the sequins caught the lights on the dance floor. "Perfect," said Valentin. "You are the birthday girl and now you look like a real folk dancer."

Valentin took my hands and put them on his shoulders, then he placed his on my hips. We moved from side to side with the music as other couples took to the floor. It seemed an eternity until the music sped up a little to a more regular rhythm and by then, Ana had a partner too, a young lad with slicked back hair, and a white open-necked shirt. He had grabbed her when the music was speeding up. She seemed to know him.

Valentin swayed me from one side to the other to the music. It was pretty simple to start with until he wanted to swing me round in a circle, in a *csárdás*. "I feel dizzy!" I yelled.

"Keep your eyes on my shoulder, don't look at anything else," he said. "You'll be fine!" We slowed, stopped and turned to swing around in the other direction. "Help! I have to stop!" Valentin stopped us and put my hands on his shoulder once more and we stepped from side to side in front of each other whilst I got my bearings back. "It's too difficult!"

"You need practice that's all. You'll get the hang of it."

"And that little spin that the women do, it's impossible. I get too dizzy," I said.

"One dance step at a time," he said. "Come on let's start again. And keep your eyes on my shoulder–nowhere else–I will guide you but stay focussed. You'll be fine." This time around was easier but I was afraid to depend on him in case I fell over but maybe that was the point. Submission to the man. If he was a good dancer, it would all be fine. But what if he wasn't? Valentin kept it simple this time, first turning one way and then another. I kept my eyes on his shoulder. We stopped. "Now for the spin. When I turn you this way, try and spin on your heels," he said. So I did and I found it easy. "Now I am going to spin you, and we will have to let go. Spin around my back and I will catch you," he said. I watched Ana spin and spin around over and over with the slick-haired guy. She was amazing. So were the others. "I don't think I can do anymore for now Valentin. Let's sit down. It's good for me to watch. You can give me another lesson another time."

"Then, if you don't mind, I'd like to find another partner," he said.

"Sure," I said, relieved. I returned to the pink champagne. Not bad for an impromptu birthday. But my thoughts turned to Dany and what could be going on tonight across the border. I poured myself another glass from the wine in the ice bucket and took a sip. The dancers were speeding up even faster. Finally, the music stopped and Sonia came to my table. "Sonia! Here! Champagne! *Pézsgő!*"

"Cheers Laura and happy birthday! I have a gift for you."

"What is that?"

"You're playing next!"

"No!"

"Come on, don't be scared. You can play behind me to get a hang of it. It's a different experience when dancers are involved you know and it's what the job is for," he said.

"I hope I haven't had too much wine," I said as Sonia sat down next to me and put his hand on the back of my chair. Valentin was holding a new dance partner. "He's quite the one isn't he?" said Sonia, observing me.

"He's a good dancer."

"Yes, I saw you on the floor. You looked a little flushed."

"No wonder with all that spinning," I said, trying to cover my tracks. I could hide nothing from Sonia.

"That's not the kind of flushing I was talking about," he said, winking his eye and finishing his wine. "Now where's that viola? We need to tune up."

Soon, I was standing behind Sonia with the band, holding that viola sideways. Whilst he began a melody playing into the microphone, I played a pattern of chords and bowing he had taught me behind the other viola player. The dance floor was empty. Ana's slick-haired friend stepped forward and began snapping his fingers and slapping his legs. I kept on at those chords. I kept up playing fast, watching the dancer leaping over and over in the air until he'd had enough and received a round of applause. Then Valentin stepped forward, snapping his fingers and pointing his toes, first one foot then another. He began slapping each leg repeatedly, one after another then leaping into the air. He returned to a quieter step, clicking his fingers again. He remained in a slow tempo for a minute or so before slapping his legs and thighs loudly and with one final giant leap, both legs bent at the knee backwards in mid-air and slapping them both at once, he too walked away to a round of applause.

Another man stepped forward now, overweight but light-footed, snapping his fingers to the music. Sonia played to him directly as he jumped, slapped and kicked non-stop then Sonia stopped playing the melody and as the dancer leapt in the air and slapped his legs those final times, he played just one downstroke of his bow with each jump, no melody left and then we finished with one final bow stroke and one giant leap in the air. The dancer had beads of sweat rolling down his face, his loose t-shirt wet and wandered off to applause to drink a beer at a nearby table. We were done. "Well done Laura," said Sonia. "You are a real dance house musician now, as good as any of us."

"That was exhausting," I said. "You need to be superfit for this stuff."

"Before you leave Budapest you should support a session with a band on your own, without me. That will be the real test."

"Oh God no! I'd be terrified."

"You just need confidence. That, and practice. You can do it. I know you can."

"Thanks Sonia. I think I'm done playing for the night. I'm ready for food." I began to put my viola in its case. "It's still my birthday after all." I looked at my watch. It was eleven-thirty. "Are you hungry? Come with me to the table. My invitation. Be my guest. It's Brussels money remember." I gave him a menu as we sat down.

"It'll have to be quick, I think there'll be another session but yes, just a sandwich. Salami, thanks."

"Done. And I'll have the chicken *paprikás*," I said to the waiter, pointing at the menu with its English translation. And another bottle of *pezsgő*. Thank you."

Valentin arrived with a huge smile. "Hey! You're really getting it with the music!"

"I can't believe you are so fit on the dance floor!"

"What else is there to do in middle age?" he said.

"Drink!" I said as the waiter came with more wine. "Here, have some. Here's to me!"

"Happy birthday."

"It is. One to remember."

The band stopped finally after midnight but musicians played casually when someone bought them a beer or started to sing a folk song. Valentin, Ana, Sonia and I came out onto the square where we said our goodbyes and I slept until noon the following day.

11

Dany and Ibolya arrived home from Romania in the early evening. I had decided to cook for them after I discovered Ibolya's cookbooks that afternoon. Stuffed cabbage. They sat at the dinner table straight away. "We've got all the photos and measurements we need. I can start on Monday!" said Dany, "Oh Laura! We saw the most amazing band! Better than anything I have ever seen. Ibolya has invited them for the concert talk on New Year's Eve. I can't wait."

"What are they called?"

"They're from Palatka. A village called Palatka. I never heard anything like it."

"The trip was a success," said Ibolya looking over at Dany. "The Friday evening was too good to miss. Besides, we were able to ask out Florin, the museum curator so I've been able to invite him here for New Year's Eve too."

"Hogmanay," I offered.

"Yes! Hogmanay! We shall have whisky! Yes, Florin will bring the viola directly himself. He said maybe he will travel with the band but …" Ibolya took a sip of wine I had poured her. I had bought an *Irsai Olivér*, I fancied a white wine tonight.

"But what?" I said, pouring myself a glass.

"He said he hated New Year, but that he would make the effort for us. I think he will come. He seemed to take a shine to me," she said.

"Ibolya and Florin were on the dance floor! You should have seen them! His wife left him two years ago for a civil partnership with a transgender circus performer from The Netherlands. He's been miserable ever since." Dany was doubled over laughing. "We had such a good time!"

"He's related to Ionesco," added Ibolya.

"Ionesco is the artist, the absurdist Laura."

"I know who Ionesco is, I looked him up. I've got the same birthday as him," I said. "You know the one you missed yesterday?" Dany and Ibolya looked at each other.

"We went to his house," said Ibolya.

"Ionesco's?"

"No, Florin's. And his surname is Ionescu, by the way. Anyway, we went to his house—I can't believe you share your birthday with Ionesco, how bizarre is that?"

"Absurd, even."

"Anyway, we went to his house and there in the living room framed on the wall were pieces of Ionesco's writing. His actual handwriting framed on the wall, not copies, his actual writing."

"What did it say?"

"It was all in Romanian but Florin told us it said 'A writer never has a vacation. For a writer, life consists of either writing, or thinking about writing.'"

"That's hardly absurd. What did he say about musicians then?"

"He was quiet on music."

"Typical," I said. Ibolya left the table to go to her room to unpack some things. "So all was good then?" I said to Dany.

"I have something to tell you, Laura."

"What?"

"It's Kati."

"Ah yes, Ibolya's assistant."

"We got together." He stared at me. I stared at him.

"You mean ..?"

"Last night."

"On my birthday?" I was incredulous.

"It was Ionesco's birthday too."

"That's hardly relevant."

"We got together the night before as well ..." His voice trailed off.

"Are you in love with her?"

"I don't know. I think so. It's too early. I'm going to see her again tonight."

"So much for the birthday celebrations."

"I've already arranged to stay at Kati's tonight. You can have here Laura. Ibolya knows all about it."

"So that's why you stayed another night. And that's why Ibolya left the dinner table."

"No, we stayed for the music. And guess what?"

"What?"

"Ibolya and that Florin they really hit it off. I don't know if it was the wine but ..."

"They got together too?"

"She says, 'What happens in Romania, stays in Romania.' His wife ran off with a transgender guy ..."

"Well that is absurd–maybe ..." I sat down. "And Kati ... where does she live?"

"Out in district XII. She commutes everyday to the Ministry of Music."

"Oh, how bourgeois."

"She's from Transylvania, don't you know?"

"So it's all working out for you now," I said. I sighed. "What have you done different? You look different."

"I had my haircut at a barbers in Cluj." I looked up and down at Dany as he sat there on the chair. He was wearing shiny shoes, high waisted black trousers and a white shirt with a long collar, buttoned to the neck, no tie. "You're starting to look like Sonia," I said.

"I want to be like Sonia, he is so cool. And the band from Palatka ..."

"Sonia, he is quite something. I don't know who he is."

"He is the captain of our ship," said Dany.

Ibolya came back to the room. "Happy birthday Laura," she said. "Dany and I found this at the market in Cluj for you. You seemed so fascinated by my old phone ..." I unwrapped the box. It was an orange bakelite retro phone from Romania with a wheel dial. "Wow!" I picked up the receiver. "Hello Romania! Hungary calling!"

12

December arrived with a full moon. A fresh flurry of snow dusted Pest rooftops white like the sugar sprinkling on a chimney cake. Christmas lights were on full along the length of Andrássy Avenue. Even the old building at number thirteen had coloured lights on the scaffolding that faced the street. One evening as I returned home, I looked up into the darkness of the black building to see Sonia's chandelier lit silvery white as full as that moon. Sonia left for Transylvania for a few days to see a family member and Dany had all but disappeared to Kati's in district XII at night, whilst working at Lajos' workshop during the day. I was left alone once Ibolya went to the Ministry of Music in the mornings and I practised the viola for hours. My playing was becoming smoother and I had regular sequences and chord shapes and chord changes off by heart. My arms, especially my left arm, had grown in strength and I could play now standing up, sitting down, sometimes my elbow propped on my knee. I could play those chord changes whilst getting up from a chair too, just like I'd seen at the Artists' Club when the music had quickened and each musician one by one in a line stood up to better play the music with such intensity. It had been so exciting to watch.

I had fallen for Liszt's second Hungarian Rhapsody in C Minor. It suited my solitary state but it was nothing like the music I was attempting to learn. Sometimes I turned the volume up on the ending and listened full blast, looking out the window to watch musicians with their instruments going in and out of the academy.

Ibolya would be home at five and we spent a couple of evenings listening to music, drinking Balaton *Olaszrizling* and cooking. "You need a new man Laura," she said the second night.

"I would have thought you of all people might say I need something other than a man, seeing as they cause so much trouble," I snapped.

"Everyone needs somebody," she said. "Come on, cheer up. You're in Budapest."

"I'm not on the lookout for anyone here. I'm here to learn about music." Truth was, I was devastated and I hadn't much of a heart left for music of any kind. What was the use of music anyway? All it did was to make me more miserable, attached as it was to every bone in my body. "You can do both," she said.

"I don't want to do both. And what would you know? You've been married to the same man all your life. You have no idea what it's like," I said. "For you it's a game because you are married. I mean, I didn't ask for this. No, I don't need another man. What I need to do is go home and get my life back. I hate Budapest."

"You don't mean that."

"No, I don't. I love it but now just isn't the time, I'm afraid."

On Thursday morning Sonia had returned from Romania and came to the apartment again. He told me he would be back the following evening for a music session with both Dany and I. He had been to the workshop and had watched the ribs of the copycat viola being steam bent into place around the mould. Dany was working now on a rough cut of the back. I hadn't dared visit the workshop what with the mood I was in and I dreaded the following day.

"You have to shake out of this Laura," said Sonia. "Let's go to the *Fonó* again tomorrow night. Maybe we can get you to play."

"It'd be good to get out," I said.

13

The following evening, I opened the door to Dany, Ibolya and Sonia. "Kati is coming at seven," said Dany putting his instrument on the floor and sitting on the sofa.

"So then we shall be five," I said, closing the door. I could barely look into his happy eyes. He was gloating over me, I felt sure.

"How are you Laura?" he said, his arms folded.

"I've been practising all week and me and Ibolya have been mooching around the apartment in the evenings. How's the viola going?" I asked suddenly remembering the reason we were in Budapest. "I've got all the ribs in place around the mould, I've glued the spine on the back and I've glued the spruce of the soundboard too. I'm shaping and carving the back for now. Lajos is a big help. He got his apprentice to cut out wood pieces in the rough for me so I get to do the finer work. It's coming along. You must come and see it."

"I will."

"I'm very pleased with it," said Sonia.

That night, after all three of us practised together for an hour, we ate Ibolya's *gulyás* soup and Kati joined us. Single, and stuck in a foreign country with an ex boyfriend and his new woman at least for another three weeks or so, I despaired. I hated that Kati and she didn't like me much either. I wished I was back in London. We set off then for the *Fonó* and there was Valentin as I walked inside. "Laura! How are you!" I noticed the warmth in his eyes and gave him a hug. "I haven't seen you for a week."

"Here I am," I said, "and there you are too," I said to Ana as she approached. "It's so good to see you both. I've been practising my viola all week. Sonia's been to Romania and back and Ibolya and Dany had a huge adventure there too." I heard the musicians begin to tune up. "Come on," said Valentin, "let's dance." So I did.

I bought a beer for Ana midway through the evening and we sat to watch the other dancers. I noticed her father with a new woman. "You like him don't you?" said Ana.

"No, I'm just fed up for now." I could see Kati and Dany at another table, their arms around each other. Dany had no concern for my welfare. "It's horrible here. I wish I was somewhere else," I said.

"Don't worry, Laura. You have a friend here in Budapest," and she put her hand on mine. I was touched. "Why don't we go somewhere else?" I said. "I never did get to The Little Pipe. C'mon, the trams are still running, let's go and get a late night bite. I'm fed up with all these star-crossed lovers. Even Ibolya's flirting like mad over there."

Snow was falling heavily as we left the *Fonó*. We braced ourselves against the wind and took a tram back over the Freedom Bridge. I stared up at the night sky through the window, watching the snow fall. We got off halfway along Rákóczi Road and made our way along a black Acacia Street, sparsely lit with yellow street lights, red neon from shopfronts and white falling snow.

Piano music was emanating from The Little Pipe. "It's that song again," I said as we entered. *Those Were The Days*. "It's the Russian guy Vladimir at the piano. I saw him at the Artists' Club on my first night." Inside we took a table for two close to the piano. It had a traditional, old-fashioned air, white tablecloths, ice buckets, mirrors, chandeliers, dark heavy wood fixtures and fittings, portraits on the wall. It was a warm, busy little place with a pre-war feel. Vladimir was playing Chopin now, I noticed. I grabbed the menus. "Come on Ana! This is on me! That European money is for us tonight! Stuff the rest of them! I'm so cold I think I need soup again! Let's have the *gulyás* soup! And Bull's Blood."

"Yes, me too! But it's half past ten!"

"So it is–well, we'll have until midnight I'm sure. What a great little place. Everyone looks important in here. I wonder who they all are?"

"Maybe they're spies," whispered Ana.

"Tell me about New York," I said when our soup arrived.

"That's where I'm from!"

"Do you miss it?"

"In a way, but I like it here. It's easier somehow, quieter. New York is so busy." I reached for a *pogácsa* that had arrived on the table. "Yes, I feel like I'm back in time someplace. And that I've become an aristocrat," I picked up my retro wine glass and took a sip of Bull's Blood. Ana laughed and joined with me, clinking our glasses.

"So–how much do you like my father?"

"Oh, stop it! I'm not here much longer you know? I've got enough dealing with Dany and Kati. Anyway, what about you and that guy with the slick hair?"

"My dad doesn't like him. He says I need someone with a good job, not a lousy folk dancer who works in a music shop."

"Don't you just hate dads? What's his name anyway?"

"Ádám."

"He's rather good on the dance floor, I noticed. And he likes you. Here's to Ádám," I said and held up my glass to hers.

"Here's to Ádám," Ana replied. I stared at the piano for a moment.

"You look really sad," said Ana.

"I am sad. I think I might ask the pianist for a request. What do you think?"

"What will you ask him for?"

"Something happy."

"A waltz!"

"Oooh! Or something Hungarian!"

"Not Bartók …"

"God, no. Something upbeat to cheer us up."

"Maybe something Christmassy," said Ana.

"Yes, something Christmassy to cheer us up and written by a Hungarian composer! That's what I'll ask for!" But I couldn't think of anything happy by a Hungarian composer right at that moment. "I think I'll ask the pianist when there's a gap in the playing," I said. "Are you hungry enough for more food?"

"How about a pudding?"

"Pancakes! Let's have pancakes! Ooo and a glass of Tokaj! The sweet wine. I know, I'm going to buy the pianist a Tokaj and then I'll ask him to play something cheerful. He's stopped now." I ordered pancakes from the waiter and asked him to bring us and the pianist a Tokaj. Vladimir looked over and raised his glass. "*Egészégedre!*" I said. "Cheers!" He came over to our table.

"Thank you for the wine," he said.

"You're not Hungarian?" said Ana.

"I'm Russian. My name is Vladimir," he said as he held out his right hand to Ana. He took her left hand and kissed it. "*Csókolom*," he said. She beamed. He took my hand too. "*Csókolom*." I beamed too. He was charming.

"Vladimir," I said. "We wanted to ask you to play something Hungarian, something cheerful and something Christmassy but we weren't sure such a thing existed. What do you think?" He pulled a chair from another table as other diners were leaving. "May I join you for a moment? I am on my break. Now let me think …" He held his glass to ours and we took a sip of Tokaj together. "Those composers, they don't always like happy music," said Vladimir. "Maybe I can play a little Brahms for you."

"Laura needs cheering up. Her boyfriend has found someone new," said Ana.

"And I have to stay here for another month and put up with it," I said.

"Now I understand. So you are here for Christmas. Look!" Vladimir pointed at his watch. "It's nearly midnight. If I'm going to play for you, I'd better do it now. Ladies …" He left us and sat at the piano. Ana and I looked at each other. The restaurant was emptying out and I could see it was still snowing outside. I heard the piano begin to play, it was a bright little march. What was it? And then I heard it! Of course! It was the Nutcracker Suite, Tchaikovsky. It was superb! Ana and I were thrilled. What a night! Vladimir played well past midnight and when he had finished, we leapt to our feet to clap.

"That was amazing!" said Ana.

"Thank you so much. You've lifted my mood completely," I said.

"It is my pleasure ladies and, of course, my job. I always play light romantic music for the customers."

"Are you from Moscow?" asked Ana. "I'm Ana by the way."

"I am from Moscow and you are from, let me guess, New York?"

"How can you tell?!"

"I've never been to New York but I've seen it on the TV."

"How long have you been living here?" I asked him.

"Twenty years. I play, I teach music. I used to teach Russian except nobody wants to learn it anymore. They wiped it off the school curriculum so …"

"So now you play every night?"

"Not every night."

"Wasn't there a famous piano player here? You know, the one who never left district VII in ten years?"

"He did leave in the end. He killed himself. Yes, he wrote *Gloomy Sunday*."

"Ah! That's the song!"

"He survived the war and came back and he wrote the song … and The Little Pipe is now famous."

"I must say, I like its old style."

"We came here to escape," said Ana.

"I came here to escape," I said. "I came here with a boyfriend to learn music but now he has found someone else. I wish I could go home but I can't until after the New Year. I'm glad we found you."

"I'm glad you found me too," said Vladimir.

"I'm glad I've found you both!" said Ana.

We stumbled out long past one o'clock, snow falling heavily. It was quiet. I felt free with my two new friends, free to be myself in these empty streets. This was a safer time, a slower time, and that beautiful Danube with its glorious bridges–one, two, three, four–on that glorious bended river–downriver Vienna–we were in a place where neither neurosis nor capitalism had fully got us. It had got me by the throat in London. But as in all mass societies, there was still a place to hide. Civilisation had its discontents, but I had left mine behind–for now.

"I always feel Budapest is more beautiful in the night time," said Vladimir, "and even more so in the middle of winter. You can keep the sunshine as far as I'm concerned." We walked through the snow to the Franz Liszt statue.

"You know, I can see not one but two Franz Liszt statues from Ibolya's flat," I said. "What do you think of that, Vladimir?"

"At least it's not two Karl Marx. Then, I would be worried."

"You're funny, Vladimir," I said, my head turned to the sky, catching snowflakes on my tongue.

14

Project 'Find Zoltán' and Valentin and I were off to the *Fonó*. Deák Square was crowded with young people sitting on the grass and drinking and there was a Gypsy busker there playing violin. We stepped onto a stationary tram 47, validated our tickets and sat down. Where was Zoltán? Houdini was Hungarian but it seemed that Zoltán had also done a disappearing act. The only place I could find him was on Facebook. Where the hell was he? Why hadn't he responded to my message two weeks ago? I made up my mind to leave if I couldn't find him. It was easier now. The east was open and would never be closed again. I had resolved things as far as I could. And for tonight, I would hear Palatka again, perhaps for the last time? I wondered as the tram cluttered towards Buda over the Danube.

Palatka were about to play. I bought Valentin and myself a beer and stood by the side of the stage. All seats were taken. I scanned the room for Zoltán's hat then forgot about him once the lead violin, or *primás,* took to the stage, playing a slow melody. Another musician entered playing violin, joining in as he walked on stage. Then a viola, then another viola, then that double bass whose timing stopped for no-one. Another violin, another viola, another double bass. I counted. There were three double basses on stage.

This was more than one band, this was maybe three, an orchestra of sorts and the music filled the hall in layers of sound. Young men took to the platform in waistcoats, hats and boots leaping in the air, slapping and kicking. When I realised my glass was empty, I looked around the room again for a hat but there was none to be found. I heard the compere say the word *'furulya'* or flute and decided to leave the ethnographic details to the ethnographers and headed back to the bar.

Where was Zoltán? I had watched the show for over an hour. I waited a little longer to cool off then re-entered the hall. Every musician and dancer from the show was on the stage in a choreographed frenzy. Even the *primás* had taken to the floor now for a show of dancing.

Still hot, I went back to the bar when the concert was over and watched the crowd. The musicians came out one by one with their instruments, talking, having a cigarette and a *pálinka* by another smaller stage at the bar. Valentin came over. "I'm going to leave when the dance starts. It gets too noisy and I won't be able to hear the music. I never did get the hang of the dancing, you know," I said. He shook his head in disbelief.

"Give me one dance. You need it. You're too much in your head these days. Why did you bring your dance shoes all this way? You're wearing them after all. Come on."

The musicians stood and each took a chair from the back of the stage and sat down in a row and began to play. Suddenly, the floor swamped with people. I held Valentin by the shoulders and we found our way into a slow, irregular movement to the music. It allowed plenty of time for conversation, exactly what this part of the dance was meant for, to flirt and charm your partner. "How is it working at the Artists' Club?" I asked. "It's good. It's regular work, there are good people there. I get to dance and I get to have a normal life. You remember when I was 'low profile'?" I laughed.

"I remember when both you and Ana didn't have your papers, yes. How long did it take you?"

"About ten years."

"That's so long, but why?"

"No-one asked and when I was asked for my papers, I went and got all my papers. So now I am the normal guy with the normal job. I am a good catch."

"But you don't want women anymore."

"No. I have sown my oats. Some Scottish oats as I remember."

"Ha ha ha. I remember." I raised my right eyebrow. "I like the new improved Valentin. You're calmer now."

"I have all my papers. I have all my cards. I am a worthwhile member of society. I pay tax …"

"OK, I get it," I said. "But where the hell is Zoltán? I thought he was obsessed with dance like you are."

"He is. We will find him. He can't be that far away. You know, for a while Houdini used a trap door in all his acts. It was a stage he was going through. We will find him." The music quickened to a slow then faster *csárdás*, making conversation impossible. We danced for twenty minutes and at the end, I was breathless and I said, "What's with the Houdini joke?"

"At times such as these, some humour is required."

"You're crazy," I said, laughing.

"Your dancing has improved. We shall find the mighty Zoli, king of the dance floor, and you will get to dance with your king."

I left Valentin at the *Fonó* and walked to the tram stop. It was past midnight, still hot. On the tram, I opened the window wide and stared up at the sky and the stars and the lit bridge. It was beautiful. I walked back from Deák Square down King Street, surprised to see so many still out on the streets. I was beginning to give up on Zoltán. There was no way I was going to hang around in my past, nor in my present for any man. What was it I did wrong?

Nothing, I decided. I had waited twenty years for my past to return and I wasn't going to waste another minute. No. I was going home.

I turned onto Franz Liszt Square and saluted the Liszt statue in my mind. Liszt and his large hands were made for women. Laura McLove, lover of musicians and dancers alike, had stuck her neck out for love like Franz Liszt but Liszt had many lovers and admirers whereas I myself had none. Zoltán had thrown me a line and disappeared. What was to become of me? Go home. Turn back. I believed in the great love of Zoltán The Magnificent but currently he was doing a magnificent job in being nowhere to be seen. I looked up into the night sky, imagining Zoltán The Great had many lovers. He deserved a constellation in the sky. He was a dancer. He could have anyone with that hat and style. I didn't know his second name, even. All I had to offer were my memories. I clung to them like I clung to the dream that I belonged here in downtown Budapest, where the youth of Europe were now converging, opening up old tenement blocks with their bars and their art. It was always beautiful down here but there was something in the air now. A quiet takeover, not a frenzy of development. There were plenty of boarded up buildings still. It was a town in transit. From communism once, to not quite capitalism, yet.

The crisis of the banks was wrecking our inheritance, our shared European consensus. Perhaps capitalism wasn't the answer. The powerful possibilities following the collapse of the Wall had been stalled. Now new walls and fences were going up all over Europe and a slowing down was taking place. I liked this in-between town between old and new, retro and modern. What was this rush for the future? Here in Franz Liszt Square, I could still fancy myself as the lover of men, as the lover, the muse of the great folk dancer, Zoltán. Who was there to tell me otherwise? No-one. No agony aunt, no specialist, no psychiatrist. No-one could see me here with their western eyes, they who were so busy with getting ahead. I could create myself as I saw fit, hidden from view. The right had lost the culture wars and there was a freedom for me in that. No more marxist alienation.

I took the lift up to my fancy oligarch apartment. I poured myself a glass of *juhfark* from the fridge. I could see the lights from the Buda hills winking at me in the distance. The pendulum was swinging once more. Perhaps capitalism should be dropped in the dustbin of history along with psychiatry and therapy and treated with the contempt it deserved. One seemed to cause the problems that needed relief from the others. Happy people don't need psychiatrists. Anxious people do. Was it all just a failed experiment? What had I really come here for?

15

The next day was colder and darker than the day before. Ibolya had the heating on full. I took a lesson with Sonia at number thirteen in the morning and in the afternoon, Dany and I practised together. I tried to explain to him about the Russian pianist but he had no interest. "I'm here for Hungarian music," he said. "Although I'm not sure why we are bothering to learn this stuff anymore." He hadn't spent a night at Liszt Square in a week but he made it clear that he wished to have the room for himself again. Kati's place was far out in district XII and he was fed up with the commute. We continued to practise but I could see his mind was elsewhere.

Ibolya was tiring of the tension. "I'm not being horrible, but I have work to do and I need to keep Kati happy and … is there nowhere you can find to go? It's only for a few weeks," she said. "Kati and I could get on with some work in the evenings. To be honest, I'd like the place to myself." I began to stay out as much as possible in the evenings. I hung out with Sonia at the *Szerb* on Saturday eating my first Serbian chicken dish and spending the night on the sofa at number thirteen, I hung out with Ana at the *Mérleg* on Sunday. By Monday morning, instead of practising on my own, I went to Klauzal Square to check on the viola being made. Vivaldi's *Winter* was playing in the workshop. Dany wasn't there but Lajos was, Bartók asleep on a bench. Where was Dany? I asked him. He's not coming today, he said. They've gone to meet Kati's parents in a fancy restaurant over in Buda. "It must be getting serious," I said. He saw the look on my face. "Come on, let's go to the New York Cafe. I'll treat you to a coffee," he said.

"But isn't it called the *Hungaria*?" My face brightened. "I've always wanted to go, I just haven't got around to it," I said.

"It'll always be the New York to me."

"Can you show me the viola before we go?" I said, looking around the workshop.

"Over here." He swayed his right arm and pointed at the corner bench. "He's making great progress. The ribs are glued to the back over here and he's shaping the soundboard. He'll be cutting the '*f*' holes later in the week and look,"–he held a block of maple in his hand–"this will be the scroll."

We set off for the New York on the corner of Elizabeth Boulevard and Tobacco Street. It was a magnificent building. The hotel towered over the street, the cafe on the ground floor. "I think we should have dressed up Lajos," I said.

"No, this place is for everyone. All the artists and writers–they didn't have money. You know, even the early film stars came here," he said. The ceiling was huge, painted with angels, giant pillars lined the room and we took a table beneath a huge mirror.

"How come you know Sonia so well?" I asked Lajos. The waiter handed us a menu as we sat down.

"Our families knew each other from way back," he said. "We were always making and fixing up their instruments for them, rehairing the bows. The old music never goes out of style, not completely. You know, those old classical composers, like Liszt, they always had deep connections and friendships with instrument makers. It's no different for us. It was no different back in Romania."

"I never thought about it. I suppose it makes sense. And which town was it?"

"*Sászrégen*. That's Reghin to you in English. The communists built a factory there but it was really a guild of instrument makers before. Musical instruments were the cutting edge of technology at one time, you know. Even Stradivarius came to Transylvania to buy his wood."

"Really?"

"Sure. There's Italian Valley nearby. The story is this is where he got his wood. The best spruce in Europe."

"Gosh, you know a lot."

"I know this. It's time for coffee. How about a Dob cake? It has seven layers."

"Sounds terrific," I said, handing back the menu to the waiter. "This place is incredible." I looked around the room. "It's not used by artists any more is it?"

"It's not the same. There aren't the numbers in Budapest anymore. All this grand architecture, it's from another era."

"It's like wandering through time. And yet … there's an abandoned air. I like it. No-one's been trying to fix it up, you know, keep it up to date, gentrify it. And thank God for that."

"I don't think the communists believed in gentrification," said Lajos. "That would be anathema to them. The term wasn't invented in 1945."

"Goodness! Look at this cake–only seven layers! It looks like more!" There was a caramel crust topping to my cake slice, layers of cream and chocolate and as I took a bite I tasted walnuts and coffee too. "Whoa! This is unbelievable! I feel like Empress Elizabeth!"

"It's the best Dob cake in the whole of Budapest!" said Lajos. "And the coffee's not half bad either."

"I met Vladimir, the Russian pianist the other night. It was at The Little Pipe–you know it?"

"Of course I know it and I know the pianist too."

"He said that a famous songwriter used to play there."

"Rezső Seress, yes. My grandfather knew him. He also played at the *Kulacs* around the corner. My grandfather left for Israel, but Seress–I guess he loved district VII. And he wrote Gloomy Sunday." He took another bite of cake. "He never did leave district VII in the end. He could have gone to America and got his royalties."

"No wonder he was gloomy. I love these stories. I love these layers to Budapest," I pointed to the cake. "There's a people's history everywhere. It's just here, waiting to be discovered."

"Devoured," said Lajos and we were quiet for a moment as we finished our cakes.

"I need somewhere to live for a few weeks Lajos. Do you know anywhere? It's why I came to see you to be honest. Ibolya is getting fed up with me and my relationship with Dany …"

"I understand. You know I have a bed I keep at the workshop in case I have an emergency job on … if you get really desperate."

"Really? Wow, that would be cool."

"It's a bed rather than a room. I mean, there's a kettle but you can't cook and there's no bath. Still, I'm sure we could work something out for a night or two if that's what you really want."

"I've got a sofa at number thirteen too," I said. "At the square," I added.

"Interesting place that," said Lajos.

"Yes, but who owns it?"

"I have no idea. And I have no idea how Sonia lives there. I mean, he earns a living but he's not wealthy."

"He is sovereign to himself," I said. "I've never met anyone like him. Ever." Lajos laughed. He was pleased I was impressed with one of his oldest friends.

16

Budapest. The town where nostalgia *is* what it used to be.

Valentin had asked to meet me downtown at *The Trapartment*, an old communist prison cell turned event venue where tourists could be locked up and attempt an escape.

I asked Valentin when I met him at the door, any sign of Zoltán? but he hadn't seen him. "Maybe he's out of town?" he said, as we sat downstairs in the prison cell beneath the streets of district VII. A guy was playing Irish folk music on the sound system for *Tilos* Radio–Forbidden Radio. Everything had turned on its head these days but there was something rather intriguing about the whole scene downtown. It was alive.

London and only money was sovereign. The people weren't sovereign because they were priced out of housing by China, international finance, Russian oligarchs, Arab oil money, you name it. The regular people were priced out and now the suburbs, now the home counties, further and further the crisis stretched with more and more regular people priced out and the irregular people–the ones who couldn't be bothered to actually live in London–were priced in. There was an explosion of aspiration around the globe, so it seemed, and all were to descend on the south east of England, by hook or by crook. How in hell did everyone get aspirational all of a sudden? And all ended up living in socialist housing masquerading as designer apartments.

Housing shortages were widespread after the war, but London saw fit to create a housing shortage without one. It had declared war on its own citizens, unlike Budapest where downtown was awash with crumbling apartments of a spacious grandeur. One housed a postman, another the teacher. No end of consumer products filled shop windows now, but so far I hadn't seen a burkini for sale.

So France suffered London's housing crisis, Berlin suffered London's housing crisis and a refugee crisis, and I was suffering from my own crisis. Why did everyone have to be on the move? Two generations ago we stayed in our home towns. And amongst all these crises, politicians were having a euro crisis. Everyone was in crisis this year it would seem. How many more crises could we take? Could we all calm down for a while?

There were more lesbians in Hackney per square kilometre than anywhere else in Europe in the 1980s but were there any lesbians in Hackney anymore? They had all gotten married and moved to the suburbs. The cultural cleansing was almost complete.

I had come to Budapest to sort out my identity crisis. Maybe it was another one of my bonkers ideas but frankly any idea seemed like a good one right now. In Budapest under communism the workers were sovereign, that's why they still lived in the main districts. If democide was death by government–two hundred million in the twentieth century–then London had been killed from rentocide–death by private landlord. There would soon be no reason to visit London at all, it would be turned into one giant gated community.

We had an inner sovereignty that winter, slaves to no-one and masters of our musical destiny. We reigned as royalty whether we deserved it or not. No kings nor queens remained in this part of the world. We ran across the streets of Budapest, with its odour of petrol and dill, its dance halls and music clubs, sovereign in our own right and in our own minds. We shone a light on ourselves, in the darkness, in the depth of winter in the snow, deep in the heart of Europe, an undiscovered gem of a place. I was queen in those few weeks, Dany king and Sonia? Emperor.

I had changed. I was no longer a sophisticated metropolitan, if I ever was. I had become unsophisticated. I had walked off in the opposite direction and I was glad of it. It had been a transportation back into time. A time of art nouveau, the beautiful for no reason other than it was a joy to look at, music for no reason other than it was a joy to listen to and love, yes love, for no reason at all. Modern people were stupid anyway. They couldn't grow a lettuce or fix a broken chair.

Sovereignty–what was it good for?

Socialism for the rich and capitalism for the poor, that was the new western Europe. Austerity was bogus I reminded myself as I passed the *Szimpla* Garden later on my way home. I was beginning to understand why Rezső Seress didn't leave district VII for ten years. The seventh district was an axis of music. The *Szimpla* on Mondays, the Grid Garden on Fridays, the Artists' Club always and just on the border there was Franz Liszt Academy.

The beer was cheaper here. I decided maybe I didn't want to leave either. This was home. Budapest–where the rentier capitalists hadn't arrived yet, but I had. I fumbled in my pocket for a hundred forint coin–no German euros here–and flipped it in the air. Heads. I heard Franz Ferdinand playing from inside the *Szimpla–'Take Me Out'*. I decided to stay, in a place unneutered, where the people, the music but especially the dance itself was still sovereign.

If the city was the reflection of its inhabitants, what was London? Wealthy, corrupt, never more than one foot away from a rat, with sewers of fatbergs beneath the streets. What was Budapest then? It was shut on Sunday. Thank God, for that. The homogenisation of the west, its music, its wine, its people and food, took no refugees. All had to become one in the city.

The city–the core of our neurosis. Health was never to be found there, in its gyms and yoga classes, in its swimming pools, in its mindfulness meditation groups. Health was found in nature. The city was a cathedral to the intellectual mind, the one that created problems only to solve them, usually badly. Freud had lived in Vienna, after all, not on the land. And in a pre-Olympic run-up Budapest, don't forget the local Roma are the ones who keep your rents down. Don't let the investors turn your town into a sterile void of trendy metropolitan gastrophiles and super rich, who don't appear to have much taste. They turn every town into a wealthy dormitory with a few left behind to clean the toilets. At those prices, a musician couldn't spend that much time being bohemian. The malignant neoliberal orthodoxy had eaten bohemia in the west. Only middle class private school kids could afford to rebel and buy a guitar these days.

Fortunately, most of my fellow maze dwellers were wholly unaware of the escape route. They thought everything happened in London, maybe New York. But there was too much happening, that was the trouble. We were all on the same slope and it was a slippery one. Greece scapegoated to the south, bombs and gunmen in Paris, Brussels, Berlin, and a flowing of people desperate to get in. I was desperate to get out. Where was safe? the Artists' Club.

A warehouse of souls someone said, but we were a dancehall of angels. Freedom–that's why people came to big cities. Sex, freedom from ties, and money. But we weren't free in the west anymore if we ever were. The consensus had changed. A couple of decades of London bombing and street harassment and I had had enough. But the movement of people and things and ideas was becoming unstoppable. I was a privileged case and not everyone moved from a sense of privilege. I didn't feel guilty about it. It's just the way that it was.

Borders. What were they good for? When did music respect the border of a nation? Music was music. Like a bird, it travelled on the wind, in the airwaves. Music of the village, long abandoned, out of fashion, reborn here in a city of diamond light.

Most had no idea that music lived and was unbounded. Technology had seen to that. It was now in the realm of the special few, condensed in the matrix of intellectual thought. That's why everyone looked bewildered by Budapest in the west. But Budapest had talent, yes Budapest had the X factor and down here in district VII, we were still young, we were still free.

17

I got a letter from Sam. The cat was fine. The flat was cool. He said he loved me and when was I returning? And could I send him some money? He said that his friend the artist had thrown him out when he was too drunk one night and now he was living at The Void but could he stay over at mine? He was becoming a living work of art, like Gilbert and George, he said. Only he was a living, breathing poet not a painter. He had written a poem about being homeless and read it at The Void's poetry slam. He had written another called Cosmic The Donkey. He had been getting drunk every night and Tracey Emin had been round for a nightcap. When she saw his bed, she thought he was making an artwork. He was living giro to giro, he said, but the SS (Social Insecurity) were giving him a hard time. They had no time for poets in England, not unless they were sponsored by the Queen.

I started to worry about Sam taking over. He was taking over my life in London and I was losing my life in Budapest. I was in a radical transition, a no woman's land of love and everywhere there were enemy lines.

18

Another night on Franz Liszt Square and I knew it was time to go. Tuesday night I stayed at number thirteen and by Wednesday, I approached Valentin about my predicament at the *Fonó*.

"Come and stay with me! I'm house-sitting for a woman up in the Buda Hills next week right until after New Year. You can spend Christmas with us! She leaves next Wednesday and the house is huge. She lives there all alone but she's going to Transylvania for Christmas and won't be back until the New Year. Why don't you come?"

"It's just what I need. Thank goodness."

"Then, it's decided."

"Oh, thanks Valentin." I gave him a hug and I felt a strange feeling come over me. I had forgotten about love what with all the other problems I was having. I was experiencing my own unique migration crisis.

Next morning, I made my way to number thirteen before Ibolya was up. I told Sonia of my plans to move to the Buda Hills. He nodded with approval. "You'll have some peace of mind up there. It's rather beautiful. And you'll get to to travel around more and see the city from the other side of the river. It used to be a separate town, you know."

"Lajos and I lived it up at the New York yesterday."

"You mean the *Hungaria*. You went to see Lajos?" He smiled. "He's a great guy."

"We were wondering–who owns this building? How come it's such a wreck? It does seem odd that in the middle of town, such a beautiful place is left nearly empty–and yet, here you are living here. Does anyone know you're here?"

"Yes. Of course. I'm like a concierge for the place."

"You are?"

"Sure, the place would be completely empty if it wasn't for me looking after it. I get to report back …"

"To whom?"

"Actually I don't know who owns the building, but I do keep a lookout for it. Its an arrangement. A friend I know."

"You are a mystery to me Sonia."

"I'm going to teach you some new chords today, Laura." He picked up my viola and played a complicated sequence of chords, including minors and sevenths. There were a lot of changes.

"I don't know if I can learn all of these complicated things. Does that mean you're teaching Dany a new melody?"

"It does. It's good for you. You have to push yourself or you'll get complacent."

"I don't think there's a risk of me becoming complacent. I'm being shoved from pillar to post. Dany is waltzing off to Romania and is all loved up. I sometimes wish I was back in London. At least I had a man there who was interested in me."

"He's a poet. He's unreliable."

"You're all unreliable. You're none of you any good for me." Sonia handed me my viola. "I told you I would teach you what I know. It's what you wanted."

"The only reason I stay here in Budapest is for you. We made a promise to help you but you don't need me anymore. Dany is doing the real work."

"I like you Laura. You need to relax more. Look around at all the good things in your life." I walked over to the window.

"There's never not someone with an instrument case crossing the square," I said. "Have you noticed?"

"It's good to know there's musicians about. It makes me feel like I belong," he said.

"It makes me feel happy," I said. "I love music."

He wrote out a list of chords and chord shapes, lines with dots on, where I should place my fingers for the chords. He took his own viola out of the case and we tuned up together. It brought a smile to our faces. Music echoed around us creating a wall of sound.

I started with a D major, then slipped my middle finger down towards the scroll until it sounded minor. It was awkward to hold but manageable. G minor next then all the way through the scale. E minor, A minor but the D Sharp note! Some of these chord shapes would involve lengthening the muscles in my fingers. And that would take a week, I reckoned. "I'll let you practise them for a couple of days," Sonia said, "and then I'll show you a simple sequence or two. It's one thing holding the chord, it's quite another to change from one to the other and keep the music in time and keep the chords in tune," he said. He picked up his violin. "Here's the tune, it's a morning song to wake people up when they've slept after a wedding party." I looked out the window listening to the slow melody and wiped a tear away. "Laura," he said. He stopped playing and put down his violin.

"It's the music, it's beautiful," I said. "I just feel so sad." He put his arms around me and gave me a hug. He looked me in the eyes and said, "Laura, you have to move on. Maybe it's good you will have Valentin for company. He could be just what you need."

"Would you meet me at The Gourd? I haven't been yet. They have music there …"

"Sure I will. They're great guys down at The Gourd. They play old style down there. I love that stuff. When shall we go?"

"Tomorrow? Brussels research so my shout."

"I will be your guest."

19

That afternoon, I decided to visit Liszt's house on Andrássy Avenue. It was at the old music school. He lived in three connecting rooms overlooking the avenue on the first floor. There was a grand piano in the central room and then several others, along with a small, austere oak single bed. Liszt was a womaniser. He had big hands, I could see, from the cast of his hand in a glass cabinet. I saw that austere bed and wondered how he could have managed all those mistresses on that little bed. I noted that he took visitors only between three and four in the afternoon, he was too busy composing or teaching or having mistresses at other times. I imagined him on a snowy evening, walking along Andrássy Avenue to the music school, his home, his big piano hands swinging, his hair swept back, his mistresses on his mind. I wondered if Gustav Mahler had popped round between three and four on a winter's day, trudging along through the snow on the boulevard. Would he have taken a tram? He would have walked to the old academy and knocked on the door of the great composer and lover of women, Franz Liszt. I imagined the two romantics drinking tea and discussing music. Afterwards, I walked past *Művész*, the artists' cinema, and decided to go in. They were showing a Béla Bartók documentary with English subtitles. It was three hours long.

I called Valentin when I got out. Would he meet me at the Artists' Club? Bring Ana! Bring anyone! I rang Ibolya too.

"Did you know that Liszt only received visitors between three and four in the afternoon?" I said to Ibolya that night at the Artists' Club. "Oh, and by the way, Béla Bartók was a folkie."

"He was a modern composer but he used the folk idiom. Most people think that folk music is inferior to classical because it's not written down …"

"So it's like trickle down economic theory?"

"In a way … except it's trickle up in this case."

"Let the rich create more wealth and it will trickle down the economic scale … except it doesn't work."

"No, it's trickle up–same as music. Folk is not a degradation of the classical, there's just a whole different world going on."

"Bartók, he was trickle up all the way," I said.

"Bartók was an exceptional man," said Ibolya.

"Anyone who could write a book and call it Romanian Folk Music volumes I II and III needs his head examined," I said.

"Maybe he loved his work."

"Jazz was folk once, was it not? The banjo came from Africa. There's a bagpipe …"

"Forget about bagpipes. It means nothing. It's the intellectuals and the musical dwarfs who categorise music. You can't categorise music. It's all simply music."

the Artists' Club was extra busy. I had my usual of stuffed pancakes to start followed by chicken *páprikás*. "Let's a have a *kékfrankos*, a blaufrankisch," said Valentin. "Let's experiment a little. There's a *kékfrankos* from Sopron here. Shall we order a bottle? It's got more cherry flavours than deep summer fruit, it says here." He was reading the menu.

"Summer seems like forever away," said Ana. "Can we have the *kékfrankos* Laura?"

"Sure, it's not me that's paying anyway–it's Brussels. Who'd have thought that twenty quid could buy dinner for four? Not me, that's for sure."

"I heard from Florin today," said Ibolya. "He wants to come with the viola on New Year's Eve. We need to find him somewhere to stay. I will have Dany and Kati at mine. I don't think number thirteen is a good idea, if you know what I mean."

"Maybe he could stay up at the Bartók House?" said Valentin.

"I never thought of that. It's far away."

"It's a bus ride, that's all and it will be near to Laura. Laura could look after him."

"Does anyone stay up there? I thought it was a museum?" I said.

"It is a museum but they sometimes have researchers from other countries to stay. It's a big place. I will ask at the Academy."

"What else did he have to say?" I wondered as I held my glass out to Valentin for some wine.

"That he was looking forward to seeing us, that's all. Here's to Europe," said Ibolya holding up her glass.

"Here's to Europe," we said in unison, glasses in the air.

"I've never eaten out so much in all my life," I said. "I could live like this forever."

20

"Would you please play an 'E' so I can tune out from it?"

Dany and I were having musical differences. Sonia's complicated chords were getting me in a fix. I couldn't hear anything properly. I could no longer detect whether one note was higher or lower than another if they were close. That made two of us out of tune. "This sounds terrible," I said. Dany threw his violin onto the sofa. It was then I noticed his shiny black loafers. "Look at those shoes! You've gone Gypsy!"

"That's it Laura. I've had enough."

"I can't help my playing. I'm doing my best," I said.

"I'm leaving you."

"You've already done that," I said.

"I mean, I'm leaving London to live here. For good. I can work anywhere with an instrument workshop. Lajos said he will help me and Kati and I are getting a place together. Maybe I can even join one of Sonia's bands." He was smirking. It was all working out for him. "I don't think you're that great at music to be honest. It's not like you come from a musical family."

"Said who? And it's not like you did either sweetie."

"I'm not playing anymore."

"So what do you want? We asked Sonia to show us what he knows. The viola is coming along, no?"

"It's all going very well. I'll be finished by next week. Then we just need to sort the varnishing ... Lajos has a few secrets for that."

"I'm fed up with the way you've been treating me. I've done nothing wrong, even Ibolya got fed up with me ..."

"That's your fault."

"I've had to sleep at number thirteen sometimes! I've had to stay out of the way of Ibolya and eat out all the time."

"I noticed you were putting on weight."

"I have to go out to eat again this evening. I invited Sonia to the Gourd. The guy who wrote *Gloomy Sunday* played there and I haven't been yet."

"I want to see Sonia. He's my friend too."

"You do as you want." Dany left the apartment.

"I'll be at The Gourd at seven," he said as he walked out the door. I heard the lift open as I looked out the window. It was nearly dark.

By seven o'clock, we were seated at The Gourd. It was on the other side of Elizabeth Boulevard, cavernous and cosy. It was early for music but there was a giant cimbalom–like a decorated piano with the lid off–in the corner and musicians were putting on red waistcoats. "How was your day?" I said to Dany whilst looking at the menu. "I think I'll have stuffed cabbage for a change and *kékfrankos*."

"I went back to work on the viola," said Dany. "It was all good." Sonia–in a white and crimson floral shirt, giant cuffs and collar–came to sit down after chatting with the musicians.

"Laura is having trouble with those new chords of yours," said Dany.

"I am having trouble with them–maybe I should stick with the easier style?"

"If you start to learn the difficult style, then the easier style will get even easier," said Sonia. "Stick with it. You don't have to play in public if you don't want to, remember," said Sonia as the musicians began to tune up. A wave of soft stringed notes wafted around the room from the cimbalom. I watched the player hit the strings with soft ended sticks. It was lovely. "This is restaurant music, it's easy on the ear whilst you're eating," said Sonia. "It's not what I would choose to play but these guys, they're good musicians."

"I love the sound of that cimbalom," I said.

We poured two glasses of *kékfrankos* and clinked. The waiter approached for our order. "I'll have the stuffed cabbage please?" I said and handed him the menu.

"And for your son?" said the waiter. Suddenly I noticed that the music had stopped. I stared at Dany. He stared back. It was clear to both of us. The nagging age gap. The awkwardness in company. We would never survive this. "I'll have the goose," he said.

I sat in silence. I deserved better than this. I needed someone who had my back not someone who was undermining me. He was lost to me now, I knew, and he sat there silently raging. At last, the band started again and the waiter brought dinner. The food was good but we ate in silence until Dany made his excuses and left and I was alone holding a glass of *kékfrankos*. Sonia was joining in with the band.

It was the last meal I had with Dany. It was sombre. It was Monday. Gloomy Monday. A swift *pálinka* with Sonia before I left, alone.

Trudging through snow down Acacia Street on the journey home, I heard piano music coming from The Little Pipe and decided to go in. It was ten-thirty. There was Vladimir. The restaurant was nearly empty. It was Monday, after all. Gloomy Monday.

"Laura! How are you?"

"I've just been to The Gourd. They've a cimbalom band there, it's all very Hungarian but it's not as posh as here. I liked it. I'm on my way home."

"Come and have a drink with me. There's *pezsgő*–it was left by a customer. Sit yourself down."

"And how are you?" I asked.

"Just the same. Working most nights. Playing my piano. I'm happy enough."

"That's Moscow weather outside."

"In Moscow it's even colder," he said pouring me some fizz into an old style champagne glass.

"Oh, this is wonderful! I'm so happy to see you! I feel like I'm really living sometimes here in Budapest, you know? Dany is coming to live here, he told me. Him and Kati ..." I sighed and took a sip of champagne. "Will I ever get over it?"

"Never mind him and Kati. What about you and me?" I stared at him and then I laughed.

"Me and The Russian!" I raised my glass to clink with him. I loved Vladimir that night. I felt like I belonged in these surroundings, in the rougher part of town and this is what I loved most about Budapest. Here we were in the gutter, feeling like we were stars.

He took my right hand and I joined him on the piano stool. "I have something to play for you. It might suit your mood. You're right about those Hungarian composers, they don't like happy music. See if you can guess who this is." He started to play *Consolation No 3* by Liszt but it was no consolation at all. I clutched the glass of *Törley* in both hands and tears fell down my cheeks.

He walked me home to the square that night. It was beautiful. We stood under the Franz Liszt statue and kissed. I looked up at number thirteen and thought I saw someone at the window but just as I looked the light went out.

21

Next day, I had to clear my head. I walked through the square past that statue of Franz Liszt and his giant hands held to the sky as it began snowing again. How I hated Christmas! I thought of Dany and his age. I couldn't blame him, he was too young. I thought of his mediterranean looks, all the gay men in London that came onto him. In Budapest, the situation was reversed–all the Hungarian girls came onto to him and he saw himself as a great catch. I walked away from town this time, along the boulevard from Oktogon. I marvelled at the Christmas lights, the dirty buildings, the trams, the cars, I marvelled at it all. I marvelled at the sound of the traffic tuning up like my favourite musicians. I marvelled at the trees that lined the boulevard, black as soot, same as the buildings, only some bright spark had thought to wrap Christmas lights around their sooty trunks and the thought that someone–a bureaucrat–had thought such a beautiful thought to lift my sad heart on a lonely winter's day broke me open. I stopped on the *Teréz* Boulevard and leant against the wall.

You weren't meant to be this beautiful, Budapest. We forgot about you after 1956 and left you here adrift, the ugliness closing in. Left to linger in a stagnant hell but still your heart is greater than the sum of all the other European hearts because–like Cinderella–you had to hide your gold. Your heart with your snow and your music and your Sonia and I cannot bear it because I am sad when I should be happy and your beauty and your suffering cuts through my centre and all the time a melody is playing in the background of my mind. *Consolation No 3*. I began to curse music and melody, symphony and harmony, Brahms and Liszt. Those songs that appeared from nowhere I had learnt never appeared from just nowhere. Somewhere in the banks of my memory, in my cells, in the blood that surged through my body and connected to my soul, somewhere in my memory, every emotion was stored through music and every time those emotions wanted to speak, they picked a song and sang, "Pay attention." So why should I pay attention to you, stupid melody from my soul? Couldn't you disappear for a while? It's not as if this isn't painful enough without a soundtrack. I forgot of course at that time, that in a happy state, I could forget myself as I walked along, begin whistling and humming, not caring who heard. In those happy states, happy tunes came forth so my thinking mind shut up. The snow was falling heavier now so I picked myself together and, as I did, I raised my eyes to the building and saw there a plaque. Gustav Mahler lived here, it said.

22

It was time to move up to the Buda Hills. I hadn't seen Vladimir since our kiss but my heart was heavy with other matters. I gathered my things and my viola and took the bus up to Pasareti Street, past leafless trees and houses that looked haunted. There'd been a thaw so it was damp–unusual for Budapest–and I saw a solitary black bird fly across the sky. I made my way to Bud Street. The house had a turret and stood alone in a garden surrounded by black fencing and hedge. I opened the squeaky gate and walked up the path then climbed the stairs to the front door. I saw that the curtains were closed.

I heard a crow caw as Valentin opened the door in a dressing gown. He looked dishevelled.

"A good night at the dance house?" I asked.

"It was great but it was very late." I saw a woman walk across the hall behind him wearing a large white shirt.

"You have company," I said. I was cursed by couples.

"Come on inside." He took my bag and led me in the hallway. "We're in the kitchen. Would you like coffee?"

"I'd love a coffee," I said, following him through the kitchen door. "Is this dress down Saturday? And can I join in? I'd like to stay in bed for a week at the moment," I said to the woman in the white shirt at the table. "I'm Laura. I saw you at the *Fonó* the other night. Pleased to meet you." I held out my hand.

"Pleased to meet you. You are very welcome," she said as we shook hands. "My name is Natalya."

"You're Russian? That's a lovely name. Do you live in Buda?"

"No, Pest actually. I heard about your troubles. Poor you–but there is a room we prepared for you here and you are very welcome. And if you want to sleep for a week, I think you've come to the right place. Nothing happens up in these hills."

"I really appreciate this," I said to both of them as Natalya poured me coffee. "I couldn't stay with Dany any longer, it was making me miserable. And he's so happy right now. I hate my life."

"Don't be like that." Valentin stretched out his arms and gave me a hug. "Come on, we made up a bed for you. I'll show you. And tonight we'll light a fire and drink some wine and Natalya is cooking for us and then you will sleep well and everything will look different in the morning."

"I hope so. It's good to have a change of scene," I said, looking around.

After coffee, Valentin and I climbed two floors and up to an attic room with a sloped ceiling. A dark oak bed with patchwork quilt and white pillows dominated the room, and there was a fireplace with two pewter candlesticks.

"Can we light the fire?" I asked Valentin. "It's so lovely," I said, crouching at the fireplace to take a look.

"Sure," he replied, "we can get it aflame for you. This room is a little chilly right now."

"And look at this quilt! It's amazing!" I said, as I felt it with my fingers. "It's beautiful."

"It's from Transylvania."

"Whose house is this again exactly? Because these aren't your things."

"Her name is Báthory."

"No!"

"It is!"

"You cannot be serious!"

"Her name is Éva Báthory. I met her at the dance house."

"You had an affair with her?"

"No."

"That makes a change."

"She's older, she's a widow. She wanted to visit family in Transylvania and asked me to house-sit to look after the place. She'll be back in three weeks."

"It's a beautiful place. A bit spooky though."

"It's old, that's all."

"Well, thanks for taking me in," I said as I opened my viola case. "I think I'll use the time to practise the viola. I'm beginning to get the hang of it." I held the viola in place, plucked the strings–it was in tune–and picked up the bow. I played some chords–G, C, E, A. "What do you think?"

"You're getting it. Keep going and don't give up. Soon you'll be playing at the dance house again," said Valentin as he began to light the fire. "I already prepared this last night." He took a single match and lit around the paper and kindling. It caught fire in minutes.

I spent the afternoon practising those same chords over and over. G C E A. G C E A. G C E A. When I got fed up with G,C, E and A, I lay back on my bed to think. I was a long way from home. I felt like I was out on a limb up here in these hills away from downtown. I felt my loneliness closing in again as darkness fell. I put more wood on the fire and pulled up an armchair. I lit the candles and became hypnotised by the flames. My mind stopped at last and I had peace.

Dinner that evening in the dining room. Sleepy eyed, I walked downstairs and entered the room. A central chandelier was lit over a dining table spread with a white embroidered tablecloth. Two red candles were aflame and only two places set. White plates, silver cutlery, wine glasses including some retro champagne glasses. There was a carafe of red wine and an ice bucket with a bottle of champagne in. "Wow," I said to Valentin. "I think I need to dress for dinner." Suddenly awake, I ran back upstairs.

I opened my case and dug out the only fancy clothing I had–a crushed black silk dress. I put my hair up and put on my diamanté earrings. Finally I slipped on that black embroidered sequinned waistcoat that I bought from the old peasant woman at the Artists' Club. I descended the stairs to dinner hearing the champagne cork pop and feeling like Anna Karenina.

"*Pezsgő* Laura? Champagne?" said Valentin.

"*Igen*," I said. "Yes."

"You look beautiful."

"Thank you. I really need to hear that right now. Where is Natalya?" I asked.

"She had to go."

"Why?"

"She has a date with her fiancé?" He looked at me with a grin.

"Are you serious?" I laughed and sipped the champagne. "God, that tastes good! Look at it sparkling under the light!" I held the glass high up for the chandelier light to shine through it. "Thanks Valentin. I'm so glad I'm here." He picked up his glass and clinked with mine.

"To your health," he said.

"To our health."

"To our health." We both took a sip. "We have everything we need. Natalya cooked us borscht and made pancakes this afternoon, we have the open fire to keep us warm, we have champagne, we have some great food and we have company. We can relax and be happy." I sat down.

"It feels very grand. It's a different world up here in the Buda Hills. It feels a little isolated in a way," I said.

"It's not downtown. This is where people bring up families and grow gardens."

"Do you prefer it here?"

"So long as I live anywhere in Budapest, I am OK," said Valentin.

"How did you know this was your home when you came here first?"

"I just knew, that's all," he said.

"I wish I could be happy in one place …" I sighed. I held up the glass of champagne to the light once more and took a sip. "This is the life!"

"Cheers!" Valentin got up and went into the kitchen. He returned with a white tureen and a ladle and proceeded to serve me the blood-red soup. "And now for Bulls' Blood, it works well with borscht," said Valentin pouring me wine from the carafe. "You've thought of everything," I said. "Are you in love with Natalya?" I asked.

"Sure I love her."

"And the fiancé?"

"He doesn't seem to mind," he said.

"Seriously?"

"It's different here, people marry because everyone marries. Everyone has affairs, it's called communism. We share things around."

"I don't think that's what Karl Marx had in mind," I said.

"Marxism is a theory, here in Hungary we put it into practice–in a good way," he said.

"Are you seriously telling me everyone has affairs here?"

"Not everyone, not all the time but it's not unacceptable. People marry to become adults–then, you are free! What else is there to do when Big Brother controls everything? Besides, what's the point of all those great Turkish Baths if you can't get naked once in awhile."

"I'm shocked."

"You'll get used to it," he said tearing into some bread. "How do you like the soup?"

"I love the soup. The colour is incredible. Natalya knows how to cook."

"She's my girlfriend," he said, nodding in satisfaction.

"I don't think I could live like that. Do the women like it?"

"Natalya likes it. She has a fiancé for her future security, and me to keep her happy. We are all fine."

"Are you saying that capitalism has brought the privatisation of love, of the couple?"

"I'm saying that when your freedom is curtailed somewhat, you have to make the best of it. Besides, there's been no great women's movement here. And we like it that way."

"*You* like it that way, you mean," I said.

"I go with the flow. I like it anyway. I'm married, remember? Also remember this–Elena Ceausescu was head of the Romanian Women's Committee."

"'Nuff said." I sipped some more Bulls' Blood.

"Did you know your daughter is in love with Ádám?" I asked him, changing the subject.

"Seriously? Now I'm the one who is surprised! She told you that?"

"She told me that. Do you mind?"

"Of course I mind! He works in a record shop."

"He's a terrific dancer ..."

"She needs my permission."

"Ridiculous. She's eighteen years old! And you love dancing. I mean–what?"

"You talk like her mother." I threw my spoon on the table.

"What?"

"Here in Hungary we have a different way of going about things."

"*You* have a way of going about things but what's game for the goose …"

"It's not called the wild east for nothing." Valentin began laughing now. "So we are weirdly somehow related! You are her Budapest mom. Well, we may as well get used to it," he said, raising his glass.

"Cheers. I suppose I don't have to feel so alone then," I said, picking up my spoon and finishing my soup.

"Let me show you a dance step before we are too full to dance. Come on, you have to dance as well as play that viola," he said standing up. He put a record on–it was the easy dance from a little village called Szék. We stepped forward then backwards to the music and then he held me whilst I danced around to the right side and back, and to the left side and back. I put my hands on his shoulders as we began to turn a *csárdás*. My spirit lifted for a moment then all of a sudden, we stopped. Our eyes met and I could feel him closing in. "No, Valentin," I said. "It's not what I want." I stepped away. "I've had a great evening, it's so good of you to look after me." I walked towards the door. "I need to sleep. I'll do the dishes in the morning, leave them there. Goodnight Valentin, you are a good friend." I closed the door and climbed the stairs to the attic, got into bed and fell into a deep sleep.

23

Living with Valentin was comfortable at first. He had an unusual diet and subsisted on corn flakes and white rice without Natalya around. "Why don't we have vegetables with the rice?" I said as I went to the shops one morning. "You need some vitamins as well as energy." The kitchen radio was tuned permanently to *Folk Radio*. As I steamed some vegetables for us one evening, he began to talk about his childhood in Romania and holidays with his mother to Transylvania. "Tell me how you left Romania?" I asked.

"I took the train direct to Vienna with my wife, then I went to the American Embassy. It didn't take long and it wasn't so difficult."

"You're a defector!"

"Yep, after ten days, they flew us to New York and I stayed in America for twenty years, New York mostly," he said, laying plates on the table.

"What about your wife? You're still married, right?"

"I love her."

"You do? I thought you loved Natalya. How can you love everybody? Ah, I remember," I said, lifting the pan off the stove, "love means something else here in the wild east."

"She got fed up with my affairs, to be honest. Anyway, it was good to bring Ana and her brother to Romania to meet the relatives. Her brother went home but we decided to come here. There was a woman in Bucharest making a car trip and I fell in love …"

"God, not another woman!"

"No! With Budapest. I was home, I realised."

"You never want to return to Romania? I've heard it's beautiful there." I dished us both steamed broccoli and rice and returned the pan to the stove.

"It is beautiful but I changed in America. I'm a liberal now. I believe in sexual liberation. The Romanians … the mindset. It works for me better here and I can visit when I want."

"You mean the communist mindset? Not everyone has that."

"You don't know how bad it was." He held his knife and fork vertical in each hand, his fists on the table.

"No, I don't. It's true."

"It messes with your head. I had to leave my family. I had nothing. No money, nothing. And now I don't fit in anymore anywhere. Romania is a ridiculous idea."

"Why so? Does that make you ridiculous?"

"No, but the borders … they changed over and over, and it's the mindset …"

"That's the same for a lot of countries, especially around here." I stepped out of the kitchen to the hall. I needed to pee. He got up to follow me.

"I'm not Romanian anymore." He was right in my face now.

"I need to pee," I said stepping into the bathroom. "The food's on the table, I'll be back in a minute." He followed me into the bathroom.

"Romania hasn't changed just because the dictator's gone. It takes generations to clear that. That old guard, they still go on about the great Romania."

"Could you stop following me around this apartment talking about Romanian nationalism? Talk about a conversation stopper. We're going out to hear the most beautiful music in the world tonight." And at that he smiled and returned to the kitchen.

I kept a little distance from him that night at the dance house.

24

I needed a new music teacher. Sonia was too far downtown to come daily and was getting busy in the run up to Christmas. Dany was in the workshop day and night completing the viola–early next week, he said–and for the all important work of varnishing. The instrument would also need to be played in–where all the parts of the viola would start to move and shift subtly until finding its stability and tone.

Valentin had introduced me to László at the *Fonó*. He was the spitting image of Karl Marx. He had asked me how much music I had studied and when I replied that I was self-taught, he sighed and sipped his beer. He wasn't keen on women musicians but he was keen on my European funding and agreed to come the following day at noon.

The next day, László arrived dressed very much the part of the music teacher in a grey overcoat and hat, a grey suit beneath and a grey bow tie. We played together for two hours, one hour spent helping me master those complicated jazz style chords and another, running through a simple suite of melodies. László's playing was loud and clean and bright whilst I was so out of tune at times, I sounded like an old-time Transylvanian peasant, he said. I didn't take it as a compliment. "You would think it would be easy to play a few simple chord shapes over and over." He was tough on music, tough on the causes of music.

"Getting three strings in tune over and over sideways is impossible at a speedy rate." In tune? Out of tune? The thing was to keep playing as no dancer would care so long as you didn't stop playing. And that was the hard bit–could you play for the best part of an hour? Standing up? Elbows in the air? Old men could do it but could I? The answer for now was no.

We had tea and cake afterwards when Valentin came in the room. "It's so wonderful to have music in the house," he said. "Next time, I might start dancing with you."

"You might have to wait a while for that to happen," said László, before biting into a piece of *Zserbó* cake.

25

Early Sunday, I left Valentin listening to *Folk Radio* in the kitchen and took a walk down to the Bartók House on Nettle Street. I pressed the buzzer and the gate swung open. There was no-one. I walked up the winding pathway, past a pond and a life-size statue of Béla. How strange it must be, to have your own statue outside a house that you once called home.

A woman opened the door then took me upstairs. There was a grand piano in one room, now a concert hall but the two other rooms were where Bartók lived and composed. Transylvanian textiles and old-style furniture with wooden carvings filled the room and there, in the corner, was the Edison phonograph. Thomas Edison was frightened of the dark so he invented the lightbulb to shine a light downtown but he must have loved music to invent a recording machine. Could he have imagined the great composer Béla Bartók heaving this bulky piece of technology around Europe to record music of the peasants? Who listened to Bartók much these days anyhow?

I left the Bartók House and returned home to find László already arrived. "You'll be pleased to know that I just visited the Bartók House," I said.

"Why should I be pleased?" he answered.

We began another rehearsal. It was as bad as the day before. I couldn't understand. With Sonia my playing went from strength to strength but this László–I was wondering why I bothered.

"Maybe we should stick to the easy style for now. Those complicated chord progressions are just too much for me for at the moment," I said. "Let's polish up something simple."

"Can I have a men's dance?" asked Valentin, popping his head around the door. "I'll dance in my slippers."

László began a simple dance from Szék. Easy enough for chords for me, just three–D, E and A. We played that same melody, with a little variation for five minutes until Valentin gestured he was stopping. "You're really getting it, Laura," he said.

"It's an easy one," said László, waving his hand with a dismissive air.

"What is it with the put downs László? I mean, I'm paying for a lesson not your attitude," I said.

"You're not a musician," he said, placing his violin in his case.

"Says who? You? I just played for Valentin to dance, didn't I?"

"Anyone can pick up something that simple." Valentin stared from me to him and back again, his hands on his hips.

"It was great," said Valentin. "As good as anything at the *Fonó*. Why are you being so negative László?"

"It's impossible for a woman to be a great musician," he said. "There are none in history."

"Who said I wanted to be a great musician? I'm learning for the pleasure of it."

"And you're English."

"Actually, I'm Scottish."

"You have to be Hungarian to play this music," he said.

"And you have to be a complete wanker to take my money and insult me like this. I'd like you to leave!"

"That means you hate my dancing too," said Valentin to László. "I'm not Hungarian, I just like to dance," he said. He then said something in Hungarian–it sounded like it might be swearing–and left the room.

"I'll get your money, László." And with that László left.

That night, still stranded up in the Buda Hills, Valentin and I shared a bowl of steamed greens and rice. "What were you thinking of, asking László to teach me? The guy is a music snob. A completely rigid, totalitarian, classical music moron," I said. "And he hates women."

"I thought it would be OK. I don't know him very well," he said. "Maybe he doesn't realise. Maybe he's an accidental totalitarian."

"He's a non-accidental totalitarian, non-Marxist throwback. Of all the cretinous guys I've met in London, I've never met one of those."

"Let's forget about it for now."

"How could you not know about him? I can't believe I have to go through some of this stuff and Dany is gallivanting around town, in love. I want to go home." Valentin tried to put his arms round me. "I just wish things could be different," I said.

"Then let me help you." He looked into my eyes and I felt the energy of him and yelled,

"No! This is not what I want! I want to go home! I don't even have a home here."

"Don't talk like this, tomorrow is another day," said Valentin as I ran upstairs.

I called Sonia later and told him my story.

"I don't think I'm going to last up here with Valentin," I said. "I shouldn't have come up to the Buda hills, I should never have come to Buda at all. He already made a pass at me. He says that folk dancing is like making love to a very beautiful woman …" I heard Sonia roar with laughter all the way from downtown. "And he has a girlfriend. And she is already engaged!"

"Come and see me tomorrow morning. We'll go for breakfast somewhere. I have an idea for you."

"Oh do tell."

"I wasn't going to mention it but I have a little house down at Lake Balaton. It's empty this time of year. If you ever need it …"

"I need it now!"

26

Next morning, I packed a small bag of things along with my viola and took the bus to Blaha Lujza Square. I walked along Acacia Street, passing The Little Pipe. I hadn't thought about Vladimir in days. I stopped outside the restaurant and wrote him a note:

'Vladimir! How are you? I'm going down to the Balaton for a week or so. Things haven't been going so well for me. See you very soon. Laura.'

I continued onto Franz Liszt Square and ran into Ibolya going to work. We sat beneath Liszt's statue for a while. "I'm going to the Balaton for a week. Sonia's lending me his house there and his car. I could be back on the square for Christmas Eve?"

"Then you can join me and my husband. Dany and Kati are going to Transylvania. You can have the flat to yourself until New Year because we're going to see relatives on Boxing Day," she said. "Good, it's all working out now."

I rang the doorbell of number thirteen. Sonia answered and came straight down. We walked to Klauzal Square where he had parked a powder blue Trabant. "Bloody hell Sonia! This is gorgeous! You've really looked after it."

"They're going out of fashion now but I don't care," he said. "I waited six years on a list for it. You can repair these cars on the kitchen table." He gave me a map and some keys. "I've written down the address and instructions how to get to the house. And now, time for breakfast, no?"

"Time for breakfast. I'll buy. I'm so excited!" We walked into town to the Little Bell diner on Oktober VI Street. It was cosy. Windows were steamed up from the cold and red checked tablecloths decked the room. We took two high chairs at the side bar. "Let me order for you Laura. How hungry are you?"

"Very. And there's a long drive ahead," I said.

"Then how does fried eggs, cheese, ham, pickles, jam, *pogácsa* and coffee sound?"

"It sounds like exactly what I need. You are so much fun, Sonia."

We looked at the map over coffee. "Take the ring road and cross at Petőfi Bridge," said Sonia, pointing his finger on the map. "Stay on the main road until here and turn left. You'll see the sign for Székesfehérvár. Keep following the Székesfehérvár road and keep going and you'll reach the lake." He drew his finger along the road on the map. "You might want to have a stop here for a rest on your journey. It'll be your first view of the Balaton. He pointed at the town of Balatonvilágos. The weather is supposed to be sunny the next few days. It'll be lovely driving around the lake. Tihany, where the house is, is a beautiful spot. I envy you but this is my busiest time of year."

"I'm nervous, it's a bit of an adventure, isn't it?" I said, eyeing up the food that was now arriving. "There is a phone, isn't there?"

"Yes, there's a phone. That's what I like about you Laura. Your sense of adventure. It's what you need when you are a musician." He put his hand in his pocket. "One more thing. I bought something for your journey." From his pocket, he took out something in a yellow and blue shiny wrapping. It was a Balaton chocolate bar. "Oh, I do love you so, Sonia." We laughed. "This food smells incredible."

We spent an hour talking about music and food, eating and drinking.

"What do you think of the viola with the three strings?" I asked him. "It's a one-off, isn't it?"

"I love it, this viola. It sits in the background, it supports the other instruments, it carries and holds the sound, deep and soulful. It doesn't interfere. Most people don't know it's there unless they are dancers. Then they see, and then they realise the Transylvanian music is all about the viola," he said. "I'm glad that you are learning it. It will stand you in good stead for other music, even if you never play it again."

"You really have to work with the bass when you play this viola."

"Music is work–at least for me. It's also a pleasure, of course. The viola, it doesn't show off like the violin, it never takes centre stage. It's not about speeding up and getting ahead of the others, it's not about fussy ornaments. It's about being there, just there, reliable, in the background, deepening the texture. And you'll only notice when it stops. Only if you pay attention and get tired of the drama of those top notes, you start to understand the middle ground, the middle way. And you only find this viola in the forgotten parts of Europe–it's basic, deep and rooted. We're in danger of losing the essence here, but we're not America or Australia, we're Europe, rooted in the peasant culture with its evolvement from the moon and the seasons and our immigrants of course, us Roma and our good friends, like Lajos."

If Liszt and *Consolation No 3* had me in despair, Sonia may just have been my Consolation No 4. He always made me feel good. He had the gift of friendship.

I was feeling rather retro as I drove the powdery blue Trabant against the traffic out of town at midday. It made a tinny, spitting sound and I felt an affection for the little vehicle. I crossed Petőfi Bridge–a modernist construction– and I looked from side to side to view the Danube. Those eastern cities were in a great position. Set in aspic by communism, they didn't need to get the early clumsy mobile phone–they could go straight for the slim one without the technological steps in between and they could go straight for the right answer, because we had made some wrong ones.

West of the river now, I turned at the Székesfehérvár sign and as I reached the edge of the city, I realised my mood had lifted. The sun came out briefly then disappeared again. There was a tape machine and I switched it on. *Those Were The Days*. It was that song again. I sang along to the la la la la at the end of the lines as the car spat along the motorway and my bones jostled with the car suspension. I was a fugitive from love, moving from one safe house to another but I trusted Sonia and his network. He was a good man. Besides–we had made a deal.

I arrived at the Balaton an hour and a half later when the sun had come out for good. All the problems, all of Dany, Valentin, László, all these irritations, my homelessness in Hungary, all of these things sank into the crystal water. I could have been at the Mediterranean it was such a sunny day now. I was happy. Sonia had saved the day. I parked the car and walked along the shore, humming to myself and watching the swans and ducks. How lucky I was! I bought tea and a *pogácsa* from an old-fashioned pastry shop and some groceries from a mini market, then meandered to the car. I drove back on my route briefly, then took the lakeside road to the western shore. Tihany was a little peninsula jutting out into the water. I followed Sonia's instructions and drove near to the end of the peninsula and came to Varalja Street. The house was on a little hill with a view of the lake. There were other houses behind but obscured by forested land. I parked outside and took in the view. Beautiful.

I walked up to the door, put the key in the lock and presto! My home for the week. There was a fireplace with wood and coal, a large oak table and chairs, candles and candlesticks, an old-style valve TV set, a red seventies retro phone that reminded me of the old Cilla television show with Cilla Black and that great theme she sang every week. *Step Inside Love*. I took off my boots and sunk my feet into a deep red rug on the floor and noticed plates and textiles on the walls. The kitchen was an old one, retro champagne glasses and tumblers on a shelf, white plates and heavy silver cutlery. I switched on the fridge. The house was freezing. I looked at Sonia's instructions and found the heating.

And so began my week of solitude.

27

That night, down at the Balaton, I lit a fire, switched the radio onto *Dankó* and began to prepare a vegetable stew. I poured some Balaton wine–*kadarka* from Szekszárd–into a navy blue polka dot jug to breathe. I was thinking back on all my adventures. Things had not gone well for me in Hungary. As to the cause of it all–it was Kati or, rather, Dany. Now, with both of them in another country, I wouldn't have to deal with them until nearly New Year. I was still lonely, I realised and I decided to telephone London. I could pay Sonia extra money for the call. I dialled the flat back home. It would be 7.30 pm. I could hear the phone ringing as I sat on a corner armchair and sipped my first sip of wine. It was light and spicy. The receiver picked up. "Hello?"

"Sam! It's Laura! How are you?"

"I'm drunk," said Sam.

"I'm sipping a Hungarian wine," I said. "And I'm in the country."

"I'm drinking vodka. You aren't in Budapest? How are you?"

"I'm OK. Things haven't been going to so well for me. Dany met a woman!"

"No!"

"So I'm a bit alone now. I've been all over the place. Right now, I've got a little house to myself for a week. It's like a Russian *dacha*. Sonia calls it a *nyaraló*, a summer house, but it's very warm, thank God. So I thought I'd ring and see how the cat was."

"The cat's great. Everything's the same here. I've been reading poems and getting drunk, the usual."

"I wish I was home."

"Well, why don't you?"

"I promised Sonia. I'll be back in the New Year though. Dany and that Kati woman seem serious. So I'm single again." I took another sip of the wine. "God, this wine is good."

"We'll have a party when you come back. Do you think he'll stay there? Dany?"

"I've no idea. I just don't know what's going on. I've been up to the Buda Hills. It's so spooky up there. Sonia has lent me a gorgeous Trabant …"

"A Trabant! A communist car! Can you drive it back to London?"

"No, it's his pride and joy. What a strange man he is. He lives in a dilapidated house right in the centre of town. I think the mafia own it. He guards it against the homeless or something. And then there is this violin maker–Dany's been in his workshop building this viola–I can't put my finger on it. There's something more to this. Or not, as the case may be."

"The cat misses you. I can tell. Cosmic the donkey hasn't been the same either. I hardly ever hear him hee haw anymore. The bagels aren't as fresh …"

"Oh stop it! Gosh bagels! I've been eating *pogácsa* for weeks. I'd love a bagel."

"So when will I see you? I'll get the bagels in."

"January 2nd I reckon I'll be back. Yeah, get the bagels in and tidy up the house. I wish I was there now. We could go out and see some art."

"What you gonna do all week?"

"Practise the viola? I need the peace and quiet, to be honest. Never mind the roof over my head."

"I can hear music in the background."

"It's *Dankó Radio*. They play retro magyar music all day long. It's lovely here, it would be perfect if I had company but I don't and that's that."

"We'll make up for it when you're back. What's the number? I can ring you from here if you want."

I gave him the number of the phone. "You'll have to figure out the code from your end …"

"I'll call you tomorrow–before the art shows. I'm reading at The Void again. Tracey Emin says she'd turn up."

"Your ideal woman. Goodnight then and goodnight to the cat."

"Night Laura. You haven't broken any taps have you?"

"Not yet." I put down the receiver and let Hungarian music fill the room. I took another sip of wine then went to the kitchen. I found some old fashioned bowls decorated with blue cockerels and dished myself a bowl of *paprikás* vegetables and tore some bread from a loaf. I returned to the kitchen table that I had covered with a red cloth and lit a candle. I sat by my food and said "Cheers" out loud. The wine was great. A violin began to play on the radio, a slow song. I ate my food and climbed to bed afterwards and didn't wake until 10.30 the next day.

28

Next morning, I lay in bed under the heavy floral quilt as sunlight streamed through the windows. I reached up and pulled back the curtain. Snow! Everywhere! I could see the lake but I couldn't see across to the other shore. A robin jumped onto the windowsill and as I looked down, I could see a man shovelling snow from the path next door. I didn't have to go out and I didn't have to get up. I could light a fire and cook and play. Which is exactly what I did.

I grabbed an old dressing gown and went downstairs and put coffee on first then tackled a new fire. I put my feet up and relaxed into the armchair drinking coffee and wrote a list for the day. 'Music. Cook. Bath. Wine.' There was no point at all in going out. I took out the viola and tuned it up, or out, as I preferred to think of it. I rosined my cello bow, all the while staying in my dressing gown and I began to grind through some of those simple chords. I stayed on and off like that for an hour or so, clearing out my mind of all the stresses of the last few weeks until I got hungry and made a giant toasted cheese sandwich, and sprinkled it with noble-sweet paprika. When I finally got dressed, it was 4.30 pm and I had been playing all afternoon. It was dark outside now. I pulled on an old jumper and my jeans and turned on *Dankó*. I was at peace. The Cilla Black retro phone in the corner rang out. I felt like it could be Cilla herself.

"Hello?"

"Laura! I forgot to ring you yesterday! I've been so busy. How is everything?" It was Sonia.

"It's perfect Sonia. I'm loving this telephone. I can't thank you enough. I'm all snowed in. I've been practising the viola loads today."

"Good for you."

"And I rang Sam. I miss him," I said. "I'll pay you extra, don't worry."

"So long as you're OK."

"Where are you playing tonight?"

"Actually we're playing at The Little Pipe."

"Really? I thought they only had classical music there? It must be Vladimir's night off. Good luck with it."

"I'll ring you again and make sure you're OK."

I filled a bath whilst listening to Franz Liszt–well, why not? It made an interesting contrast to my studies. I stoked the fire and pondered what to have for dinner. Noodles! Yes, noodles with cheese, salad, wine. Garlic! Yes, garlic. Oh lord what it was to please myself. I would have to go out the following day but this was like one of the best Christmases spent ever–spent entirely alone.

Some of Liszt's compositions were a little doleful I found as I was lying in the bath later. I pondered my fate. Life back home in London awaited me. It was fun, but it was reckless. And here I was in Sonia's *dacha*, or not a *dacha* exactly, that was Russian wasn't it? A *nyaraló* that's what he called it. Could it be easy being a single woman in Hungary? In Budapest, certainly. And I was an outsider so I wouldn't be expected to conform. Oh glorious music. Now I heard Liszt *Piano Concerto No 1*. It wasn't entirely my cup of tea–maybe a bit too dramatic–but the music wafted up the stairs and I wondered could you be happy in life, simply alone? Food and wine and a few good friends. I wasn't without fear but I didn't have the choice but to be who I was. And who I was, whether I liked it or not, was neither a mother, nor a wife.

When the music stopped I came out of my dream and out of the bath, pulled a towel around me, wrapped my hair in another and went downstairs. I looked at that old retro phone but it didn't ring. I put more logs on the fire. I kept the silence for once. I poured a glass of *kadarka* and stared at the flames. Tonight was for peace.

29

♥ Zoltán ♥

Zoltán remained elusive. I knew he had a special message for me. I had a dream and in that dream he appeared as a golden Archangel with two large angelic wings at his back. He towered over me in his golden hat and emanated understanding. So that was it? Understanding? Maybe that's what I needed. It's true I was confused about the past. It had been stolen from me in a way, and I needed to square that circle and move on.

Zoltán was a man, an ordinary man in all ways but one– he could dance. He held himself with an unusual grace, on the dance floor and off. For all my longing and mental projections, I knew he wasn't actually an angel. Did angels exist? I had the sense that there was a deeper purpose to my search and what better way would the purpose be shown to me, if not through music?

As I moved around district VII, or Elizabeth Town, in search of an experience with Zoltán, I realised the Budapest I once knew was being reborn. I could see it was a sticky birth but there were signs of renewal everywhere. Mainly in the bars and cafes, but also in the building works. Everywhere downtown had building works, in homes or on streets and pavements. And if they weren't experiencing building work, then they needed to experience building work. Where were you Zoltán? What is your message for me? From Facebook, I saw that he might go to the Grid Garden, a ruin bar on Friday night, so I put that date in my diary.

I was changing. I was haunted less and less by the past and, as I made a few contacts here and there with people, the present loomed closer in my mind. Then the future. The future in Britain looked grim. Out of Europe, were they out of their minds? As if last year wasn't bad enough, now Europe was collapsing both within and without. I decided to go and see an apartment on the tiny Rumbach Sebestyén Street. The building was opposite a derelict yard but up on the fourth floor, nestled a little flat with a quiet aspect onto a courtyard with those lovely wooden floors unique to Budapest apartments. It was perfect. I could have it for twelve months. Should I?

Zoltán, or no Zoltán–should I stay? I may never have the chance again and as time wore on, I fell in love not with Zoltán, who was after all a mere memory, a wisp of wishful thinking, I began to fall in love with Budapest itself. In my wanderings around the city, daytime, early evening, sometimes in the dark, I would turn a corner and tilt at buildings in astonishment. Pearl of the Danube still wasn't my favourite expression, it didn't do the city justice. A diamond was what came to mind, a dusty diamond, hidden from view. I liked the city's state of dereliction, a crumbling forgottenness, perhaps I had come here to forget myself? If I never found love again, I would have found somewhere to love, streets that I could walk on that would always astound me.

But maybe it was time to wrap things up and go home, back to the rain and the drizzle, to the Irish sessions played by English people and Germans in the pubs, back to the old rockers who should have given up long ago, back to unmade beds masquerading as art, back to the free drinks–

sure, that would be cool–and back to the chaos of the whole goddam world living in your postal district. Good for expanding your mind, great for expanding your waistbelt but bad for the wallet and bad for seeing clear about who you were and what to do. The western world was a decadent freak show. It used to be fun and now? European leaders from left to right were taking collective leave of their senses. I'd followed an inner melody back to its source. My beloved Budapest was still normal and–better–*cheap*. Those millennials could keep their 'safe space', I intended to live in one.

I had gasped one sunny evening as I walked the road to the city park. A curious building caught my eye that had a tiny bay window near its roof–it looked like it could fall off. An art nouveau masterpiece. Through the railings, I looked closer at the plaque on the wall, 'Béla Bartók College of Franz Liszt Academy,' it said.

Beauty. Here in Budapest, it was everywhere. It found you–you didn't have to seek it out. Wander and break open. I remembered another thing from my dream just then as I looked at the sun setting orange on the yellow building. Archangel Zoltán emanated his gold glow of understanding over me because inside I too carried a darkness. It wasn't an evil darkness, it was a murkiness, a dulling over. It was like a pile of dust or gravel that had been left over the open space where my heart once was.

I loved Zoltán. I knew that now. Maybe not for the man himself but for the work he seemed to be doing on the angelic realm. Angels were messengers of God–not that I believed in God as such sitting in Heaven, giving his orders. But I was wise enough to recognise that not everything that happens, happens without a meaning. In fact, everything had meaning. Zoltán the dream angel had found his gold, he wished to shine it on me. The love was still there, it had never gone away. I had to let my light shine brighter, not dimmer. I still wished that Zoltán, the humble man, would shine a light on me down here on a dance floor in district VII. Here, down here, downtown on the streets of Pest, I was finally mining some gold of my own.

There is no such thing as falsehood, merely the absence of truth and I came back to the present and the little apartment tucked between two synagogues on Rumbach Sebestyén Street and to my own personal truth. Whilst the enemies of music in old Britannia had turned on each other, they would never notice if I escaped east for good. They could keep their musical austerity. The gold was here under my feet. Oscar Wilde said a man should have a future and a woman should have a past but hang Oscar Wilde, I was a woman and I needed a future too.

Society invalidates love as a basis for decision and action but inspiration had been the spark that had ignited my quest. I looked once more around the room. "I'll take it," I said.

30

Back at the Balaton, my days fell into a little rhythm–practising that viola, cooking, walking in the snow. My playing was improving as was my state of mind.

Saturday, around six, I was experimenting with a chicken *paprikás* in the kitchen, humming along to the Palatka band on *Dankó*. There was a knock on the door. I hesitated. And then another knock. I was wondering whether to open or not when I heard a voice. "Laura! It's me. Valentin!" I opened the door. Valentin stood there in a suede overcoat, boots and black hat and scarf. "I'm freezing! Can I come in?" I stood aside to let him in.

"What are you doing here? How did you find me?"

"If I hadn't found you, I would be homeless for the night. I took the train and then the bus. Look, I've got food and wine for us." He opened his bag. I was incredulous. "I met Sonia last night. He came to the Artists' Club after hours with Vladimir. He told me where you were. He said you were feeling a bit lonely …"

"I was … I mean, it's true, but …"

"You want me to go …?"

"There is nowhere to go. Go on, take off your coat. I'm making chicken *paprikás*. I thought it would last two days but there's enough for the both of us," I said going into the kitchen. And I've got this." I held up a bottle of white *olászrizling*.

"And I have another riesling to be cheerful." He pulled a bottle of red *kékoportó* from his bag.

"My! You are fun down at the Balaton!" I said. "OK. Get warm, hang your coat, take off your boots then we'll sort you out a room–oh, and put your food in the fridge," I said. "Then we can relax."

"That's great music," he said as he hauled off one boot after another in front of the fire.

"That's Palatka."

"You've got talent, Laura. You're quite the little homemaker. This is a great little house," he said, looking around the room.

"Who's looking after the house in Buda?" I asked leaning against the kitchen door, wooden spoon in hand.

"I left Ana there. I told her I'd be back Monday. I wanted to make sure you were OK."

"And Natalya?"

"Natalya is getting married quite soon. I don't think I'll be seeing her too much anymore," he said. "It's a shame but never mind."

By evening end, the radio turned high, Valentin had his arms around me, dancing a fast *csárdás*. "Music makes the world go round," he said.

"I thought it was love that made the world go round."

"That too."

"It's making us go round anyhow." I got dizzy and begged him to stop, then he held me in his arms and kissed me. I heard a faint wedding processional on *Dankó* float up the stairs as we got into bed. Palatka again. Valentin and I were drawn into an ever closer union. He was a red in my bed, he'd become my sleeper agent.

31

Next morning, dishevelled, ravished, and ravishingly hungry. I wrapped myself in the old dressing gown, put on coffee and lit the fire whilst Valentin lay sleeping. The sun was shining, the sky blue, the sex had been incredible. I felt like a new woman as I opened the curtains–hello robin redbreast–and gazed at the lake. It was a blissful, intense Balaton blue. I started to put away last night's dishes when there was another knock on the door. Who could it be this time? I opened the door–Vladimir! "I hope you don't mind me coming to see you, Laura. I've been thinking of you."

"Did Sonia tell you where I was?"

"No, but I could guess and you said on your note. I've been here before. I rented the place a few years back for Christmas with a girlfriend. Can I come in?" I hesitated. "Is there something wrong?" Just then, Valentin appeared at my side. He was dressed by now, thankfully. "Valentin!" He looked at him, then at me, then back again. "I had no idea." He looked dismayed.

"Come in! It's good to see you. There's coffee on. How did you find us?" said Valentin. "How did you get down here?"

"I was with you two nights ago–remember? When I heard Laura left town for a few days in Sonia's Trabi, I made an educated guess. I came here a few years ago with a girlfriend. Sonia has a lot of business ventures on the go."

"He does, doesn't he?" I said. "He moves in mysterious ways." I caught Valentin's eyes as I headed for the kitchen. "Let me take your coat, Vladimir. Sit down and I'll get us all some coffee."

"I thought I'd get out of town for the afternoon," he said, putting his coat around a dining table chair. "I got up early and drove down here in two hours."

"It was a good night at the Artists' Club," said Valentin, nodding. "Maybe you could give me a lift back? I came down on the train and the bus."

I was no longer lonely, nor alone at the Balaton. I walked across a few eggshells that afternoon as we took a snowy stroll by the lake and by nightfall, I had the cottage back to myself. My head and my body were reeling from sexual congress. I was exhausted. What must Vladimir think? I lay on the sofa in silence. Valentin was a womaniser and he had taken advantage of me, hadn't he? I had stuffed it up with the Russian. I made myself a sandwich with salami and red pepper and drank green tea. That Cilla Black retro phone rang out. It was Sonia.

"Sonia! I've had Valentin and Vladimir here today. Why did you tell both of them I was here?"

"Someone needed to look after you."

"But now they've both gone. I think I pissed Vladimir off–we kissed the other night and then he found me with Valentin … it's a mess."

"Don't worry, Laura. You're on holiday, remember?"

"So you had a good gig on Friday night? You all stayed up late at the Artists' Club, I heard."

"Ibolya and her husband were there too. She sang a couple of songs, you would have loved it."

"I'll be back at the square on Wednesday … I'll drop the car at the parking for you …"

"And you will come to mine on Christmas Day–it's decided. Ibolya says she is having a little evening with you on Christmas Eve. We'll be one happy family on Franz Liszt Square. We shall take care of you, Laura. OK?"

"OK. Thank you Sonia. I haven't been lonely at all. And I've got two more days for music practice."

"Bring some of that nice Balaton wine with you," said Sonia. "I'll call you Wednesday and remind you to lock everything up."

"Goodbye Sonia. I'm falling asleep here on the sofa. It's been good."

32

Christmas Eve and I drove easily into Budapest against the traffic despite the snow, the powdery blue Trabi chugging and choking my bones homeward. At dusk, I crossed Freedom Bridge decorated with Christmas lights. The Danube was black, inky, reflective. I sang aloud to Palatka along Rákóczi Road, Berlioz's old Hungarian anthem, then took a turn along Acacia. I passed The Little Pipe, I took a right down King Street, past the brazen lights of the Liszt Academy on my left and crossed the boulevard–so many Christmas lights! then parked the car at Hunyadi Square as requested by Sonia. I once again made my way back to Franz Liszt Square, this time on foot. It was beautiful. Not just the square, the whole city. Beautiful by day, glorious by night but at Christmas! It took my breath away, lit up in a glory of tiny colours from buildings, lights wrapped around trees on the boulevards, the trams even had multi-coloured lights. Who needed the daytime? I was at home once more.

Ibolya was in with her husband when I arrived. A Christmas tree was lit in the corner by the window. "Lajos was here earlier," she said. "The viola is complete. And the first varnishing is done. It's all on target."

"What of Florin?" I asked. Ibolya looked at her husband for a moment but he was busy reading *Magyar Hírlap*, the daily paper. "He's coming on New Year's Eve. He's officially staying at the Bartók House but I expect he will also stay here."

"And is he bringing the instrument?"

"Yes, he's bringing it. The musicians are arriving that day too. Sonia has found them a place at number thirteen. I can't wait. It's going to be a ton of fun," she said, holding a cigarette in her mouth with her right hand, a lighter in the other.

"I still don't understand why you are doing all this."

"Because I can," she said, then took a first puff.

"I have something for you," I said. "I had quite a time at the Balaton let me tell you but on the plus side–here." I handed her a box wrapped in gold paper. "I stopped at the *Törley* place in Budafok on the drive back. Did you know Joszef Törley was the first man in Budafok to own a motor car?"

"*Törley Brut Nature*. Fantastic," she said. "I'm always in the mood for champagne. We can drink it tonight."

"I've got another for Sonia for tomorrow. I'm going to number thirteen for a Roma lunch. Should be interesting," I said, sitting at the dining table.

"Indeed," said Ibolya as she walked to the kitchen leaving a waft of smoke behind her. I heard the fridge door open then close as she put the bottle of wine inside.

33

Christmas morning and I headed for Sonia's. He was wearing a white shirt rolled to his sleeves, open-necked for once, and a grey pinstriped waistcoat with fat grey corduroy trousers. A cigarette hung from his mouth. "What's for lunch?" I asked, handing him a bottle of *Törley* as I walked through the door. "Champagne! Excellent!" he said.

He opened the door to the living room. "Everything is for lunch!" he said.

"Wow." The room was decked in red and gold and coloured lights. A main table was set with plates and glasses. A side table covered with breads, salami, sausage, russian salad, cabbage salad, cakes, stuffed cucumber. "Stuffed cucumber! You did this?"

"I love cooking. I have been cooking stuffed cabbage all yesterday but as you can see, we have everything else as well."

"Stuffed eggs! You have stuffed eggs!"

"But first we must have a *pálinka*. I have *házipálinka*, one from my village," he said as he pulled out a plastic two litre Coca-Cola bottle with a pale viscous liquid in from a cupboard. He placed two shot glasses on the table and filled them. "Happy Christmas, Laura!"

"Happy Christmas Sonia!" We clinked glasses and swallowed the *pálinka* in one shot. I felt the burn through my mouth, down my throat and the heat expanded across my chest.

"This is my Christmas open house. We call it an *itthon* in Hungary, an 'at home'. If I can't be in Romania and I can't because I have so much work, I open the door for my friends. I go and see my family on January 2nd," he said.

"With the viola this year," I added.

"With my viola. Indeed."

"You have little wooden santas on your table," I said, looking at him. "I had no idea you were so domestic."

"Here–in the wild east–cooking is a sign of masculinity. I pride myself on my cooking."

"I wouldn't have missed this for anything," I said as we looked out over the window across the snowy roofs of Pest, a shiny glimmer of icy-grey Danube on our vista. It was quiet. Sonia sighed. Suddenly tears pricked my eyes. "I love this town," he said.

That afternoon, a handful of Sonia's friends dropped by, musicians mostly, and a few with their instruments. A couple of the homeless guys from downstairs were invited in to join us too. After we had eaten, I asked Sonia why he had a woman's name?

"My real name is Sasha," he said, "but people confused me with another Sasha and one day, because I was wearing a pink shirt, someone said I dressed in women's colours and called me Sonia instead so it stuck and I don't mind."

"I think it suits you," I said. "I think you are the man for the twenty-first century."

"The century that starts next week. It has come quickly. It seems like only a week ago, we were all communists. Not that I was, of course, I just made the best of it."

"Funny, that's what Valentin said. Except he was talking about women at the time."

"Valentin is like me. We Roma got pushed around a lot, so we make the best of where we find ourselves. We don't believe the politicians too much." Squeezed between a weakened state and a global market, would Sonia make it? Sure he would. Self-assured, talented, multi-lingual, multi-cultural, multi-occupational, disciplined and yes, spiritual, how he had achieved it I never knew, but he had the courage to become his true self. He was self-oriented. He took himself wherever he went. With his grace and style, he fitted in everywhere. He was a musical oligarch. They all were. He was transnational and comfortable with it. I envied him. His identity was strong and inside himself, yet he knew what he had come from. "People think of us Roma as backward, but we are the modern tribe, we can negotiate ourselves anywhere–or at least I can. I am the liquid modern, isn't that what they say? A liquid cosmopolitan. We are eclectic, we use every resource. Soon everyone will want to be like us and some do already …"

"Dany! Have you seen his clothes lately? He's hilarious."

"He's getting it. He understands. Clothes first and then …"

"You don't become free through clothes, surely?"

"It's a statement. A statement of who you are. And no matter who you are, you can dress well and be yourself. We are a legitimate nation even if we don't have a nation state or a border. I suppose that makes me a nationalist of sorts," he said, a glint in his eye. "And with our anthem …"

"Roma have an anthem?"

"Sure we do. Even the European Community has an anthem, Laura," he said.

"Yes, it's Beethoven–no? Scotland has an anthem. We had a nation state and we gave it up."

"Incredible." Sonia shook his head. "Yes, we Roma have all the power in the world–literally–in music but none in politics." A global age of border crossings, hybrids and identity politics was upon us but t'was ever thus for Sonia. Transnationalist, mobile not bounded, open-ended, diasporic and with community across the globe, his was a lifestyle for the twenty-first century.

34

Monday and Dany returned from Transylvania alone and headed straight for Lajos' workshop. He decided to work on the instrument around the clock, eating with Lajos and his wife and sleeping over at their flat. He returned to the square in the evening to let me know everything was on plan for the viola swap, that the varnishing was going well and by Wednesday they would be stringing the instrument and playing it in, where he would play the new instrument until its sound became stable. Dany said Kati would return for New Year's Eve and he would see me then. I could tell he wanted to avoid me and it suited me fine.

    The temperature remained below zero in Budapest those days I was alone at Ibolya's. The snow wouldn't melt, the sun shone from time to time before the city plunged into its mid-winter darkness again, but alight with electric and neon colour. The streets were quieter, the academy closed for the week. No musicians crossed the square. I took a walk through the snow into town to the Rose Valley music shop and bought a Palatka CD and walked back again, watching the pigeons swoop over the boulevard as I crossed back down King Street. I was getting bored, not unusual at that time of year when everything including the length of the days seemed to be held in transit. I realised then what I needed to do: I needed to get lost.

I turned down Acacia Street instead of going home and asked after Vladimir at The Little Pipe but he was not returning from Russia until the day before New Year's Eve, they said. I decided to walk the length of Acacia, crossed Rákóczi Road and into district VIII, Joseph Town. What would I find? I found more empty streets, fewer cafes, more buildings blackened with soot, an extraordinary piece of art nouveau on Gutenberg Square. I walked past a cimbalom maker that was closed. I trudged around those streets in the snow for over an hour when a sheet of snow fell from a roof right to the ground in front of me. I had exhausted myself, my breath freezing in the air. As the sun came out, I wandered over to the Danube and found myself at the Central Market on Fovám Square. This is where people were today! I went upstairs to a food stall and ordered *gulyás* soup and bread. Clatter and bangs and doors closing and footsteps up and down stairs, a humming of Hungarian around me. I loved the market's sounds and sights and looked down over it all from a high stool and table.

I luxuriated in those few days at Ibolya's. I took myself to the New York for coffee with a notebook and began to write a diary. The end of the year was coming. The end of the century. I ventured out to a dance house on Wednesday night at the *Fonó*, running into Valentin again as if nothing had happened. I was glad of his company. He pulled me closer as the night was ending but I ran off to get the last tram. I told him and Ana I'd see them both on New Year's Eve.

I spent time reading, listening to music, thinking. I rang Sonia late one afternoon. He would be playing the evening of the concert and so someone else would have to make the viola swap. Would I do it? I was aghast. "You're asking me to commit a criminal act," I said.

"Hardly," he said. "Ibolya can distract Florin. That viola is only going back to that dusty museum. They will get like for like. They won't know the difference. I've seen it, Dany's work is amazing. I was at the workshop this morning."

"Maybe Dany should do it?"

"Someone has to. It can't be me–I'm playing–it can't be Ibolya. That leaves Lajos, you or Dany."

"I'll think about it," I said.

"Remember, you said you would help me and I've fulfilled my side of the bargain."

"What if I get caught? I'll have no boyfriend and a prison sentence."

"I'll come and see you in prison," he said.

"Thanks so much! I'll ask Dany. Kati can visit him in prison, more like."

I trudged round to Lajos' workshop myself afterwards and told Dany about the conversation with Sonia. "Yes, he asked me this morning," said Dany. "But I will be with Kati that night and Kati doesn't know anything. She thinks I'm apprenticing with Lajos to learn about varnishing and stuff. That Florin, he's fine. He's not someone to worry about," he said. "And I trust Ibolya to lure him away. I wouldn't be surprised if they ran off together."

"But she's married."

"There's no telling with Ibolya."

"So you really want me to make the swap? Why do I get the rough deal? What if I'm caught?"

"You won't be caught. It's only Florin to worry about and I'm telling you, Ibolya has him under her thumb. I'd never seen anything like it. Anyway …" he was holding the viola up to the workshop light and looking at it closely.

"It's a fantastic job," I said. "I've never seen anything quite so rough and yet quite so beautiful."

"It's a thing to have to rough up your technique. The craftsman's task is perfection, so I had to copy perfectly rather than create perfection."

"You were saying about Florin and Ibolya ..." He rested the viola back on the bench.

"If you get caught, we're all caught. It's clear you're not an instrument maker so it would all unravel for sure. But caught for what? The viola itself is of no inherent value. I know that."

"It's still theft."

"It belongs to Sonia! They took it from his grandfather! It doesn't belong to the government, the museum or that absurd Florin! The whole situation is absurd! It's a story worthy of Ionesco! I'm telling you, there's nothing to worry about."

"Then why don't you do it."

"Because of Kati," he said. "She wasn't there at the original discussion. It's too late to tell her now."

"Why?"

"Because maybe she will disagree? She'll find out afterwards but then it will all be over."

"So it is left to me then."

"I'll visit you in prison."

"But you said it wasn't a crime!"

"It's not! You have nothing to worry about. We'll all be there and if something goes wrong, we will all be found out, not just you so calm down. Everyone will be drunk at New Year and, don't forget, Palatka is playing. No-one will notice I tell you. No-one. Look at this!" He held up the viola again and it was true, it was a superb copy from what I had seen. "We made it the same weight. The same colour. The same smell. The same flaws. The same faded Roma wheel at the back. Look ..."

"It's still a risk ..."

"Laura! We both agreed to do this for Sonia! Haven't you had the best time with him learning to play viola?"

"OK. I'll do it. I love Sonia. He's the best. He made stuffed cucumber at Christmas time." When I walked back to the square, I could see dark clouds of betrayal gathering over Buda. They were heading downtown.

More snowfall that evening, pretty as a picture on the square. I listened to Liszt's *Faust Symphony* to transcend my worries, helped by a glass or two of *Törley Gala* dry champagne and some *Panónnia* cheese.

35

♥ Zoltán ♥

What we talked about when we talked about dance. Listen for the bass line, he said. I listened. I was used to listening to the melody, I had to adjust my hearing down a notch. It was a given, wasn't it? The bass line. Don't look at me, he said laughing. Look at my shoulder. I couldn't help but look at him, I was mesmerised. It wasn't that he was beautiful or handsome. He wasn't young. I couldn't place it why I had been so hypnotised. Chemistry? Yes. I could barely contain myself. Charisma. That was it. That's what he had. And he could dance. And the hat. I'd never seen him without it. When I watched him dance with a woman from a distance at the edge of the dance floor, he would bend his head over and I would see its crown. He resembled a matador then, his right arm high in the air as he turned, then he would stretch himself straight, arm still in the air, smiling because he loved it and he knew he was born for this dance floor. All the time round and round, in a *csárdás*, controlling his companion like a master bullfighter, teasing. Put your hand on my shoulders, he said, or you will get dizzy. And then he counted steps for me and I knew I had to slow before he would turn me. I didn't wear the correct shoes, I was clumsy on my feet but–

for whatever reason–he tolerated that. And now here I was being controlled by the master himself. I was weak at the knees and I loved it.

What we talked about but we never talked about dance. It was a little bit of guidance here. A little bit of guidance there. But did you know Zoltán? How much I hung onto your words as well as your shoulders. It's true, I thought I might fall. I became dizzy through turning but your height and your strength and your experience kept me on the dance floor. Nothing had–nor could have–prepared me for this.

What we talked about when we talked about dance? We never talked about it, what it was really about. *Szerelem**, Zoltán. Did you ever know? If the dance was a way of mediating female sexuality, you could mediate mine any time.

What we talked about? We talked about the old days to clear the air. There was a confusion there, who did what, and with whom. I never did dance in the old days but I remember you from then, I remember that one occasion when the chemistry was instant.

We never talked about dance. I sat there and sipped on wine and I sensed you rise from the table and I wondered and yes, there you were and you gestured that it didn't matter that I couldn't dance. It was an act of kindness on your part, a gesture of friendship. To rise to the dance floor, the only couple on the dance floor was to enter a labyrinth. You didn't know then what I felt inside. You had been on the dance floor all your life but for me it was a risk. I could fall.

*Szerelem = love

36

Florin Ionesco rang from Romania the following morning. "No, Ibolya isn't here, she's due this evening," I said. "Will you be bringing the viola?"

"Of course I will," he said.

"Then I will see you tomorrow night. I look forward to meeting you. You're officially staying up at the Bartók House, no? I'll be staying with the Gypsies at number thirteen," I said. But would there be room? I called Sonia next. "Sonia, am I staying at yours tomorrow night after the concert?" I asked.

"Sure," he said, "but, just in case, maybe you could call Valentin."

"I'd rather not … but OK. I'm going home soon anyhow." I telephoned across the Danube. Ana answered. "Hey Ana! It's Laura!"

"Laura! How are you?"

"If I'm stuck, can I stay at yours tomorrow night?"

"Sure, we'd love to have you. Your room is just the same–there's tons of space here."

"There'll be a lot of Gypsy musicians on the square tomorrow night. Maybe we won't go to bed at all. It's a new millennium."

"I can't wait," she said. "See you tomorrow night at the Artists' Club."

The night before New Year's Eve, we gathered for dinner but not at the Artists' Club. For a change–and at my insistence–we dined at The Little Pipe, the cimbalom band were playing. We had much to discuss. "The musicians will be here mid afternoon," said Sonia. "I'll collect them from the station. We'll be at the Academy at 6.30 to set up, Ibolya."

"Florin will be at mine for the night," said Ibolya.

"Why not the Bartók House?"

"That's his official residence," said Ibolya. "It means nothing. Where will you stay Laura?"

"At Sonia's or with Valentin up in the hills. I expect we won't go to bed until very late," I said. "The only problem we have is getting Florin and the viola to the Artists' Club."

"That won't be hard–trust me," said Ibolya. "I'll be dancing with him and Laura, when you have made the swap, leave for Lajos' straight after and get it to the workshop. OK? We don't want two instruments hanging around the place."

"I'll say I'm going to collect Lajos and come back with him."

"And we must carry on for the rest of the evening," said Sonia. "Like nothing unusual going on. No-one knows about this except us. The musicians won't know, so let's keep it below the radar."

"Below the radar," said Dany.

37

♥

Zoltán! You have the magic! Alas, you are nowhere to be found.

I fell into a melancholy. I could barely be bothered to search anymore for Zoli. I turned up at the Grid Garden looking for him in the late night warm spring air. He said he would be there on Facebook but he was not. The gains of my European project were being lost. Those for whom Europe had meant a loss of control, those who wished a return to an *ancien régime*, where the aristocracy, the ruling classes got to tell us what to do–those leavers had turned us all into quitters.

Through my choices, I was whirling in a downward mobility, but in that downward spiral was a place where I could call home–Budapest. the Artists' Club. A dance shared by everyone and for everyone. There were gifted dancers but none of it was possible without all of us having our feet on the dance floor. The dance house wasn't sexy–*secret-yes it was*–it wasn't popular, it hadn't migrated west, it hadn't become a free for all, watered down in cities across the globe. You had to come downtown to prove your credentials and cross the threshold that was the dance house. The greatest threshold of all–Friday night at the Artists' Club.

At the dance house, life was the opposite of the regular world. A mirror. A little bit topsy turvy, a little bit back in time.

Who owned the Artists' Club in the old days? A collective. Today, a private owner. Maybe marxism was the peasant village extended, where a group consciousness prevailed. The west had gone AWOL from the collective mind. It was our lot to invent the spinning jenny but if we had had to take a direct route from peasant to industrial, wouldn't we have chosen marxism too? We chose capitalism or it chose us, because we were shepherded bewildered into the cities and our lands torn off us and then we were told we were individuals. Sure, some of us like me became good at it. I took succour from music that was beyond borders. I loved borders though. Like an immune system–if they were strong, they would keep me safe.

Zoltán was a blank slate on which I could project all manner of a lifetime of erotic fantasy but like my life and all my fantasies, he had gone up in a state of Zexit. I walked past the Ferenc József bistro on Nagymező Street, and all the other bistros one after the other lined up with red checked tablecloths and glasses of rosé and I envied those friends, those couples. I loved the fragrance of dry hot spring air in the evening, the waft of french fries, I longed to sit with Zoltán, relaxed and happy. I sighed. I was always alone and as I had that thought I walked onto the path of a standing fan, spraying a fine mist of water around the tables and I stood there and took a light shower.

38

Friday 31st December 1999, Millennium Eve
Hogmanay

The day began slowly. Ibolya had left the apartment early for the academy. I made coffee and ate bread with jam and wandered the flat in my dressing gown. By 11.30, the telephone began to ring. Lajos first. "Laura! Is everything OK? We're all set here. I will bring the viola in a case around to yours after lunch. I'd like to see Ibolya."

"I'll ring across to the academy and tell her," I said. "I'll be here." I pulled on jeans and a woolly blue jumper. The phone again. Sonia this time. "Laura! Is everything OK? I'm all set here. I'm going to collect the musicians at three o'clock from the station. You're welcome to come and meet them?"

"I'll see you at 6.30 at the academy. I'm staying home today. Lajos is coming round with the viola after lunch. Ibolya will be at the station later too but I'm not sure what time Ionesco arrives. Maybe it's the same train?"

"Maybe …"

"You sound nervous. That's not like you."

"It's a big night. It's the millennium apart from everything else."

"I'll be glad when it's over, frankly."

"But it's Palatka playing …"

"I know … it's me that's nervous. Sorry." Just then the door opened and Ibolya walked in wearing a brown mink coat. "I didn't know you wore fur," I said.

"I wear what I like," she said. "It's minus four out there." I was still holding the receiver.

"Sonia says he'll be at the station at three …"

"I'm picking up Florin from the same train so, good, I will see him there." She took off her coat. "And tell him I've got the money for the musicians."

I waited by the window from two o'clock watching for Lajos. Sure enough, at ten minutes past two, I saw a man with a dark coat and hat, red scarf, black gloves, holding an instrument case walk across the square leaving snowy footprints behind him and turning towards our building. The doorbell rang. Two minutes later, he was standing in front of me. "Here it is Laura," he said placing the black case on the table. He opened the case.

The instrument was wrapped in crimson velvet. It was even more beautiful today. It had been dusted with rosin across the belly to look like the original. "I used some old rosin from the workshop," he said, "and we found some dust on the top of a cupboard. We mixed them both to get the aged look."

"You're a genius. And Dany?"

"He has the potential to be a truly great instrument maker," he said. "He's gone into town this afternoon. He said he wanted to do some shopping."

Six-thirty and all of us were gathered at the Academy. Florin, Lajos, Dany, Kati, Ibolya, Sonia, the Palatka musicians and myself. The talk started in one hour, the concert at 8 pm with tickets for the dance afterwards at the Artists' Club. The counterfeit viola was back in the apartment.

39

"Good evening," said Ibolya from the stage. "Tonight I wish to talk to you about music. Hardly a surprise here at the Franz Liszt Academy. But tonight I wish to talk a little about folklore." She was dressed in a long scarlet dress, a silver embroidered shawl around her shoulders, her hair up with wisps of curls framing her face. She was beautiful. I was surprised she wasn't smoking but she held a glass of champagne in her hand. Everyone had been given a glass of *Törley* when they arrived. Men in suits, some in bow ties, the women in party wear. Even I wore my little beaded waistcoat, and a long black skirt. Sonia, of course, was the best dressed of all of us. He was wearing what looked like a Savile Row black suit with black bow tie.

Ibolya began to sing. It was an old Roma song, she said. One that she had recorded herself from a village in Transylvania. She invited Florin onto the stage. "As part of my research", she said, "I discovered not only the melody and lyrics of the Roma but also, on occasion, their instrument makers. May I present to you Florin Ionescu, curator of the Romanian National Museum of Agricultural History!" There was loud applause as Florin walked onto the stage accompanied by the leading Palatka musician, the *prímás*, who carried the old viola and a bow. "We have discovered this Roma instrument, made in 1956 and brought it here to you. Florin, would you like to tell us about this instrument?" Florin looked embarrassed.

"Good evening ladies and gentleman. In truth, this instrument has been in our collection for years and had been forgotten about until recently. As you can see ..." he gestured to the Palatka *primás* to hold up the instrument to the audience, "... it is a folk instrument so it is not financially valuable as such and for this reason it has been left alone throughout the communist regime. Today, however, we look at these artefacts differently. As a relic from another time, when life was slower, where people worked the land, sang their own songs and often made their musical instruments. The instrument has no marker for its maker but we can see from the back, there is engraved a tiny Roma wheel." The Palatka *primás* turned the viola around and pointed to the button area of the back. "Which would suggest a Gypsy maker. The belly is spruce, as usual, and the back is made from maple. Although it is rough, in other words the maker wasn't a professional, we can see that he probably used another instrument to copy from as the proportions of the instrument are in harmony. We have had the instrument tuned to accompany Ibolya this evening with one of the songs she collected and learnt from her research and which she will record for the academy soon, I believe." He looked over to Ibolya and she nodded in agreement. "So now, before our New Year's Eve concert from Palatka group, I give you Ibolya ..." Another round of applause. Ionescu left the stage, the Palatka *primás* tuned the viola slightly then Ibolya began to sing. She closed her eyes and the room was silent. She sang from deep in her chest, from deep in her throat, her arms around her chest embracing herself. I heard a lifetime of cigarette smoking in that deep, rasping voice. I felt my eyes prick with tears.

The viola was harsh but beautiful, played to perfection. A round of applause followed. Ibolya spoke some more then both left the stage. The room darkened. Silence. I detected the stage curtain go down.

Three minutes later the curtain raised, still the room in darkness. I saw four lit cigarettes in the darkness as the band began to play slow. In time, the lighting raised and we could see all four musicians and a couple to the left of the stage dancing, looking into each others' eyes. Ibolya came to us. "How was it?" she whispered.

"Fantastic," I said. "The viola was amazing. Amazing and rough. It was fantastic." I looked around and everyone was nodding. "Now I can relax," said Ibolya. She sat down. "Until later!"

"Florin! Come here! Have some champagne now. We have done well." She poured Florin a flute of champagne and they clinked glasses. "Now where is that viola? We can't lose it!"

"It's there by the side of the stage," he said. "Don't worry. I won't take my eyes off it all evening."

40

Eleven o'clock and the Artists' Club was full. There were the highly dressed concert goers alongside regular dancers and also Valentin and Ana. Everyone was dancing or getting drunk or both. Everyone I noticed except for myself and Sonia who was playing on stage with the Palatka band. Valentin had been on the dance floor all night, Ana was with her beautiful Ádám–they looked superb together. Ibolya was charming Florin, looking into his eyes at a table in the corner, drinking pink champagne from an ice bucket beside their table. Dany and Kati sat near them, eating. I decided to nip home to get the copycat viola. I nodded to Dany that I was leaving for a moment.

On my return, the music had stopped and people were at the bar. Valentin came over. "Laura! You've got your viola! Are you going to play with the band?"

"Maybe … I–don't know." I didn't want to draw attention to myself. I knew Lajos was waiting for me in the workshop. I was waiting for my moment and now I needed to distract Valentin. "Valentin. Would you do something for me?" I was going to have to lie.

"Sure. What is it?"

"There's something I need to do … I'm hoping. I don't know how to say this."

"Say it. Or I cannot help you."

"It's Florin. He's in love with Ibolya. She's married. I went back to the flat and her husband rang. He says he is on his way."

"From where?"

"The western train station. He will be here soon. He's taking a taxi."

"Why don't you tell her yourself?"

"I can't. Look at them together." We both looked over at them, they were kissing each other. Dany and Kati were laughing at them. I could see Sonia looking at me from the stage.

"I will get her on the dance floor, that's what I will do," said Valentin. "I'll make sure her husband doesn't catch them."

"Fantastic. She'll be glad later."

"I can be very persuasive. I can make sure to get his attention too." Just then the music started once more. A dance suite from the Transylvanian Heath. "Here goes," said Valentin.

He walked over to where Ibolya and Florin were sitting and took Ibolya's hand, I saw him say, "*Csókolom*" and they took to the dance floor. As they did, Valentin stopped another woman, a young long-haired blond woman and took her hand too. In the middle of the dance floor, in the middle of downtown, in the middle of the Artists' Club, in the middle of the night, Valentin took two women centre stage in front of the Palatka musicians and danced with both the women, controlled them both all the way through the dance.

Florin looked on, his mouth open. It was beautiful, of course, but was akin to watching three way sex with the one you love, I imagined. I sat down at the table, nodded to Dany and placed my instrument case on the floor. There was the viola, next to mine. Florin was transfixed. I crept beneath the table and I heard Ibolya yell at the musicians from the dance floor and I opened my case. It had a simple clip fastening. I opened Florin's viola case. It was a soft case with a zip. I put my head above the table briefly. The whole room was watching Valentin on the floor with these two women. It was an astounding performance. I dived below the table again to find Vladimir there. "Vladimir! What are you doing here?" I whispered.

"I love you, Laura," he said.

"You what? What are you doing?"

"I overheard you last night. I wanted to help."

"You're not helping!" It was too late. I had to make the swap now or never. I unzipped Florin's case and swapped the two violas in full view of Vladimir. I zipped up Florin's case and flipped the lid of my own shut. It was done. The music was coming to an end and I sat up on my chair again, Vladimir next to me. I nodded to Dany–mission complete. Florin was turning back to the table. "Vladimir! Champagne!" I grabbed the bottle of pink champagne from the bucket and poured for us both, then Florin. Florin turned back towards us when the music finally stopped. "Cheers," I said. Vladimir put his arm around me.

"Cheers," he said to both of us.

"Cheers," said Florin. "That was quite the performance." Vladimir and I looked at each other and he kissed me. I was trapped by the Russian. What had he put in the champagne? Ibolya came back to the table. "It's quite a New Year," she said. "I think I'll go and talk to the band. Florin, do you want to come?" Vladimir and I were left at the table.

"What do you want Vladimir?" I asked.

"I wanted to help. I love you Laura. I don't care about the viola. It's a folk instrument. I know it's worth nothing. I heard the whole story."

"The whole story …"

"I can figure it out," he said.

"And it's worth something to Sonia. All this is for him. That's why I'm here in Budapest."

"You can trust me. I'm Sonia's friend too, you know."

"I have to go. I have to take this instrument to Lajos. He's waiting at his workshop."

"I'll come too," he said.

"No!" I took the viola, glanced back to see Florin and Ibolya kissing again by the stage, and I slipped out the door, grabbing my coat along the way and headed for Lajos' workshop, millennium fireworks from the Danube exploding around my ears, the black sky flashing above, Vladimir standing at the pillared entrance to the club watching me. The sixth district clock was striking midnight. It was the new millennium. It was the dawning of a new era.

41

All of us–Kati included now–gathered at Lajos' workshop by 2.30, still in our finery. Sonia took the viola from the case and held it in the air. "Lajos ..." he said and handed the instrument to him. Lajos placed the viola on a workbench, turned the three pegs one by one to release the strings, the bridge, the tailpiece and then the button at the bottom of the instrument.

"Are you sure it's your grandfather's viola? Not someone else's?" I asked Sonia.

"Yes, I'm sure."

"But how can you tell?"

"The scroll, I can tell by the scroll."

"The instrument maker expresses his creativity in the scroll," said Lajos. "Even a folk instrument maker understands these things and take a look inside the *f* holes." Lajos held the instrument belly to me. I peered into one of the viola's *f* holes, holding the instrument up to the light. Inside was a faint, black handwritten label:

'Lakatos Béla, Szászrégen, 1956'

"But Florin said there was no label!"

On the back of the viola, where the neck connected to the body was the button of the instrument. There indeed was a faint Roma chakra carved into the wood.

Lajos took a flat knife with a bone handle from a drawer. The edge of the knife had been filed down and was very thin. He took the knife and wedged it underneath the ebony fingerboard where it was fixed with rabbit hide glue to the neck. "Are you taking off the fingerboard?" I asked. I looked around at Dany. "But why?" Lajos turned on a bunsen burner in the workshop and held his knife edge over the flame, heating the metal. He returned to the viola. We were silent. Why this? And why now? I glanced at Sonia. He held his hand to his lips and signalled to me to be quiet. Lajos manoeuvred the knife from side to side until its edge began to make a space between the fingerboard and the viola neck as the glue melted. He continued to wiggle the knife back and forth until there was a cracking sound. We drew our breathe in unison. He stopped and reheated the knife on the burner and came back to the instrument again. The knife was penetrating deeper and deeper, the glue breaking, creating cracking noises. "We're nearly there," he said. "Dany, hold the belly a little." Dany stood forward and held the instrument. We crowded around closer–another cracking sound. Lajos stopped again and took a deep breath. "One more time and we're there." With a last deft slip of the knife, the whole fingerboard lifted into Lajos' hand. "Woo! Excellent!" I said. I was so busy looking at the black wood, I failed to see what was beneath. Sonia leant forward. "*Jaj Istenem!* At last!" He clasped his two hands together at his mouth, as in prayer. "My God."

"Oh my God!" I looked up at Dany. "Did you know this?"

"No," he said.

"Lajos?" Lajos shrugged. My mouth was wide open. I looked at Ibolya.

"Its incredible," she said. "My God!"

The viola neck was naked now. In a series of little holes drilled along the length of the neck were what looked like diamonds. "Are they real?" asked Ibolya.

I stared. I couldn't believe my eyes. I looked around the room. "My God," said Ibolya again. "What is this?"

"I never would have believed it. Not really, not until now," said Lajos. "Sonia …"

"I can't believe it's for real" said Sonia. "I never fully expected this …"

"Are these diamonds Lajos?" I asked.

"I believe so," he said. He picked up the viola and turned it over carefully. The little diamonds dropped onto the workbench. He took his bendy lamp and lit them closely, all of us leaning over the bench to look. He took a tweezer from his tools and picked up one at a time to look at them and blew his breath over them. "It's for real," he said.

"Who owns them?" I said to Sonia. "Did you know about this all along?" I asked him. I looked over at Lajos. "I knew," said Sonia, "but I didn't believe it. I did it for my mother."

"Haven't I been duped? I've just swapped these instruments like a drugs mule. This is a crime!" I was aghast. "How did they even get there?"

"My grandfather," began Sonia.

"*My* grandfather," interrupted Lajos. "My grandfather. It is all down to my grandfather," he said. "He had this viola in for repair. It belonged to Sonia's grandfather. They were good friends. But then something happened," he said. "If this is true, it must be true …"

"Here is the evidence …" said Sonia.

"What is true?" said Ibolya. "Lajos, explain!"

"My grandfather, he was in the communist party in Romania. The communists–they gave the Jews a hard time after the war. Everyone blamed them for the country turning into a one party state."

"How?" I asked.

"After the war, you have to remember there were still Jews in Europe. After the war, what other party would you join if you were Jewish? Romania was a fascist dictatorship until the very last moment, right until Russian tanks were at the border then they threw out the king and turned communist. Anyone Jewish joined for safety."

"Did you know about this Dany?" Dany said nothing.

"I ..., I ..., Lajos explained to me a week ago," he said. "I didn't think it could be true."

"*I* didn't think it could be true," said Lajos looking at us all. "It's unbelievable."

"But how did they get inside the viola? What happened Lajos?" I asked.

"My grandfather was in his workshop one day ..."

"Some Jews robbed a bank," laughed Sonia.

"They robbed the Bank of Romania, it was the only bank in the country. It had all the money, all the wages. They were insane to think such a thing."

"I didn't think that happened," said Ibolya. "I thought it was a fix up to get rid of the Jews high up in the communist party."

"Well, something happened," said Lajos. "They robbed more than they bargained for because along with the workers' wages they stole–amongst the cash–were these diamonds. I believe they belonged to the king."

"King Michael fled the country," said Sonia. "The communists took whatever was left which must have included some jewels."

"My grandfather was in his workshop. It was late July 1959. Suddenly an old client arrived. My grandfather hadn't seen him in years, he had moved to Bucharest to study music but he knew his family. Everyone knew each other in those days. He passed him a small envelope and then left. The man was very anxious and once my grandfather opened the envelope, he realised why. Everyone had heard about the robbery by then. What else was he to do? He had to get rid of the diamonds somewhere. What better place to hide them than in a Gypsy's home-made instrument? My grandfather had violins and violas in and out for repair all the time and Sonia's grandfather's instrument was getting a new fingerboard."

"We couldn't afford or even find ebony in Romania then," said Sonia.

"Yes, so my grandfather built a decent fingerboard out of maple and painted it black. It was a favour. He drilled the little holes along the neck that afternoon and glued the pieces together. My grandfather returned the viola to Sonia's grandfather the following day. He had no idea there were diamonds in the instrument, no idea at all. It happened all so quickly …"

"And then the bloody communists started harassing my family," said Sonia. "They always hated us. We earned money and had respect being musicians and so they came and confiscated our instruments. It is such a home-made instrument, they thought it was worthless which it is in truth, in and of itself. And somehow it wound up in the museum as an artefact of folklore. No-one has touched it or played it in years."

Lajos continued, "My grandfather never said anything about it to anyone until he got passage to Israel. The robbers were rounded up. My father told me this story so when I came to Budapest, I looked up Sonia's family and we pieced it together. We wanted to get to the bottom of it."

"Incredible!" said Ibolya. "I need a cigarette," she said, fumbling in her handbag. "What do we do now?"

"Put them back!" laughed Dany. "They're stolen goods," he said.

"Return them to King Michael?" Lajos looked at Sonia.

"Why should he have them? He'll hardly remember ... I say, actually I have no idea what to say."

"I know what to say," said Dany. "I have an announcement to make." He looked around the room then took Kati's hand. He dropped a bombshell. "Whilst there are announcements being made, I would like to announce that Kati and I are getting married. We picked our rings today," he said holding up Kati's hand in his. They both wore gold bands.

"Perhaps we can make you a diamond ring?" suggested Lajos.

"You knew all about this and you never told me," I said to Dany. "And now you announce you're engaged? You could have told me on your own. And what about our gig? The one in London? Sonia was going to play with us."

"It's not going to happen, Laura. It's over."

"I'm leaving. I'm going home, not that I have one here. Sonia, I'm going to yours."

"Sure," he said. "Here, Laura." He reached into his pocket and pulled out some keys and threw them to me across the bench then I walked out of the workshop into the snow. It was over. Stabbed in the front, stabbed in the back, the betrayal was complete. Dany was a musical serial killer and I was the patsy. To paraphrase Maria Von Trapp, somewhere in my distant childhood I must have done something bad. Russian roulette and Hungarian hijinks never mind Spanish practices–I decided to leave the English way. I left without saying goodbye.

Back at the square, I passed the Artists' Club. There was that song again–*Those Were The Day*s. I looked inside the door. Everyone was singing, Vladimir back at the piano, the musicians packing up and drinking *pálinka* and there was Florin, forlorn Florin. He was holding the viola case. "Florin!" He brightened when he saw me.

"Where is Ibolya? I haven't seen her for an hour," he said.

"She's coming, don't worry. She had to talk to Lajos. Did you enjoy your evening?"

"I'll enjoy it more when Ibolya returns," he said. "And you?"

"I never wish to go through another millenium night again."

42

♥

So don't come then Zoltán. Let me stew in my own *gulyás* for now.

I will pound the streets of district VII, I can enjoy this music alone, there are other dancers, other dance teachers and I am clumsy and you would look down your nose at me, would you not? Tall and proud Zoltán, you would prefer a nice Hungarian girl, not an old, useless woman like me. And yet, I cannot take my mind from you, your eyes, that hat, the way I felt when you spun me around until I was dizzy with lust and longing. I remember how you looked, tall and masterful, with grace and patience and how fevered I was! Zoltán! Do not make me wait too much more! Then I can be free of you, at least. You are exotic to me, your name beginning with a hard letter, the last in the alphabet. I hope and I am waiting. But I am not young anymore and after twenty years of waiting, I fear I cannot wait much longer.

I had survived but I was a shadow of a fallen state. Like a phoenix from the ashes–or like a melody that never dies– I had come back for a final showdown. Leave or remain? My love for Europe was strong, my love for England gone.

43

One day into the new millennium, all EC monies spent, I returned once more to London, alone. I got off the train at Liverpool Street, and walked down Brushfield past Spitalfields Market. At Christ Church, I heard music playing. Scarlatti. I went in. A group was rehearsing around a harpsichord. I left and turned into Fournier Street, the waft of curry spices a warm comfort as I took a turn onto Brick Lane, its neon signs and cobbles. I stopped at Beigel Bake for half a dozen bagels and a coffee and returned to Pedley Street. It was cold in the flat. I heard the cat mew behind the door as I unlocked it. I picked her up and walked upstairs to the living room. Sam was nowhere to be seen but the flat was tidy. I picked up a note on the table 'Laura. Gone to The Void. Back late afternoon. Welcome home. Sam.'

I sat at the table and ate a pickled herring bagel and heard Cosmic the donkey bray outside. Nothing had changed. I got out that old bakelite phone given to me as a birthday gift. It was marvellous. I plugged it in and sat it next to the lamp. I lay down on the bed and fell asleep.

For a couple of days I stayed around the flat taking stock and cuddling the cat. I ate curry and drank wine with Sam. He told me he loved me. I think he wanted to move in but I was emotionally exhausted. I didn't love him, I just needed a friend.

My music lessons had been a waste of time. The winter was still long and deep and–worse–back here in London it was damp. The clouds never lifted and by 3.30, the day was over. I listened to Liszt again, *Consolation No 3*. I shed bitter tears. I missed Budapest as if she were a person. I missed Dany too but I would never have him back. And what happened to Vladimir? What was Sonia doing right now? He would be back in his Transylvania. And Lajos would be in his workshop, going off to the *Kádár* for his lunch. And the students would soon be returning to the Academy, walking across the square in the snow. I looked outside and in the yard, some kids were burning a fire in a brazier in the yard. I went to bed early those nights, hoping for respite from my millennial depression.

The old bakelite phone rang and woke me a week later. I hadn't heard it ring in the flat before. I picked up the receiver, still in bed. "Hello?"

"Laura! It's Valentin! How are you?"

"Valentin! It's so good to hear from you! Are you still up in the Buda Hills?"

"No. Ana and I are downtown now, we have a flat to look after in Tobacco Street. It's much handier," he said. "But how are you?"

"I miss Budapest," I said. "What happened to everyone? And Vladimir?"

"You left in a hurry," said Valentin. "Vladimir is where he always is, The Little Pipe. And Ana is here, she says 'hello'." I told him about the diamonds.

"I heard," he said. "I am sworn to secrecy."

"I always thought you were a secret agent. What did they do with the diamonds Valentin?"

"They split them. Lajos took six, Sonia took six ..."

"But there were thirteen."

"Dany took one," he said.

"Dany?"

"A friend of Lajos is making a wedding ring for Kati." I sighed and fell back on the pillow.

"When are you coming back to Budapest Laura?"

"I'm not. My life is here, I can't go back and watch Dany and Kati together. I miss everyone. I miss Budapest."

"We'll always have Budapest."

44

♥ Project Zoltán and tonight I was at the Grid Garden. No Zoltán but Valentin again. It was warm so I stood outside whilst the band had a break. A woman with long hair and a floaty dress rode past on a scooter, her head held high. She stopped to talk to a thin lad in a navy shirt wearing a straw hat that looked like a flower pot. "He said he was coming on Facebook," I said to Valentin.

"It's totally clear that in times like these one should neither be hysterical nor fall into paralysis," said Valentin. "We can dance," he said. And we did.

I walked home in the small hours and I saw a lone caretaker through a hotel window. I felt sad for the world and everybody in it. I crossed King Street, stopping a moment for a cyclist with a pretty girl sitting across the handlebars with long dark hair looking sultry, sulky. Budapest was always more beautiful in the night time but I was crashing and I was burning.

I awoke late the next day. Drinking morning coffee, I opened the shutters and the window. I looked outside and on the tree were two magpies in a mating dance–one for sorrow, but two for joy. The square was busy already. It was 11 am. My flight was tomorrow when I would return to collect my things. I opened my computer and disabled the chat function on Facebook. I never had to look at that green light again. My telephone rang. It was Valentin. "I'm downstairs," he said. "The music is starting. Come down."

"What music?" I said.

I dressed and walked down the four flights of stairs into the bright sunlight. The music was coming from the stage at the corner of the square at Andrássy Avenue, the sounds so familiar. A little crowd had gathered and there were a few people in folk costumes but mainly shoppers and people sitting on walls and benches eating lunch. I walked towards the front of the stage when I saw Valentin. He was dancing a men's dance. I noticed the back of a grey jacket with black folk embroidery detail. I looked up and saw a hat. Zoltán! He turned and our eyes locked. "Laura! Where have you been?"

"I've been here all along."

"Let me give you another dance lesson." He took my hand and in my own clumsy way, I followed.

45

I had a Eurovision.

From Stettin in the Baltic to Trieste in the Adriatic, a musical curtain lifting across the continent. All the capitals of the ancient states of central and eastern Europe–Warsaw, Berlin, Prague, Vienna, Budapest, Belgrade, Bucharest and Sofia–all these famous cities. Around Europe in Reykjavik, in Paris, in Lisbon, Moscow and Tallinn, Edinburgh, London, Barcelona, Minsk–a pooled musical sovereignty. We didn't need the great leap backwards.

Borders–what were they good for?

At the Artists' Club that Saturday night, Valentin had planned ahead. My old friends–Ibolya, Lajos, Sonia, Zoltán of course, and Palatka. Vladimir was at the piano playing that song–*Aki A Szép Napok*, *Those Were The Days* ...

Yes, logic would have taken me from A to B, but there are forty-four letters in the Hungarian alphabet and it was the dance that took me back to Zoltán.

What had Budapest done for me? Everything.

Budapest was a diamond in the rough and as I danced with Zoltán again that night and many nights after, I realised a diamond, like love–and like Europe–is forever.

♫ ♫ *The End* ♫ ♫

ABOUT THE AUTHOR

When Claire Doyle isn't writing or going for a walk, she can be found trying to learn Hungarian folk dancing. Or trying to speak Hungarian. Sometimes both at the same time. Claire Doyle lives in Budapest's party quarter.

Printed in Great Britain
by Amazon